THE GUARDIANS OF LOST TIME

ORDER OF THE BLACK SUN
BOOK 48

PRESTON WLILIAM CHILD

Copyright © 2023 by Preston William Child

All rights reserved. No part of this publication might be reproduced, distributed, or transmitted in any form or by any means, including photocopying, recording, or other electronic or mechanical methods, without the prior written permission of the publisher, except in the case of brief quotations embodied in critical reviews and certain other noncommercial uses permitted by copyright law.

Publisher's Note: This is a work of fiction. Names, characters, places, and incidents are a product of the author's imagination. Locales and public names are sometimes used for atmospheric purposes. Any resemblance to actual people, living or dead, or to businesses, companies, events, institutions, or locales is completely coincidental.

PROLOGUE
THE THOUSAND SPEARS

They were going to conquer the known world and even the unknown world too. No one had any doubts about that as they marched toward battle. Their spears were held at their sides, the tips of the blades high above as they continued to move forward in formation. Those spears were the tools of change, the instruments of their intent to change everything. So far, they were succeeding—and it didn't seem like they were going to be stopped.

The gods themselves knew to stand aside and make way for their approach toward destiny.

Aegus was a young soldier in the infantry, but he made sure to carry his sarissa firmly by his side, keeping it straight so that the spear's tip shone in the sunlight high above his head. He believed in what they were doing and was determined to help make Macedonia's dream a reality. Every last soldier that was there, the lines of warriors to his right and left as well as the legions behind him, all wanted to keep conquering until there was nothing left to conquer.

His friend and fellow soldier, Fotios, marched beside him. The two of them hadn't seen many battles, but they were eager to make names for themselves. There was no better army to be a part of if they wanted to be part of battles that they could win. Still, there was some lingering anxiety as they marched into every battle, terrified that it would be their last.

Fotios stammered beside him, the shaft of his spear shaking wildly in his grip. "I hope we make it through this one."

"We made it through the last two," Aegus said, trying to be reassuring. His friend wouldn't be of any help if he went into battle filled with such dread. "So this one should be no different."

Aegus didn't really believe his own words. He had seen so many of their comrades fall around him in the first two battles that they fought in. Any one of those men could have so easily been him; if he had been standing a few feet in another direction, if he had faced a more dangerous opponent, or if he hadn't been lucky enough to avoid the arrows that rained down on them. In the thick of those battles, any single little moment could be the last. He just hoped that his luck would continue to hold. He didn't want to die, not until he had a chance to see the future that they were trying to create.

"We will make it through," Aegus said, mustering all of his courage and confidence. He hoped that he could transfer his optimism to his comrade. They both needed to be at their best to watch each other's backs and to survive to see another day. "I know we will. They say that the king will be joining us on the battlefield today. With him at our side, victory is assured."

"The king will be here?"

"He no doubt already is."

Almost as if the gods themselves were listening, everyone fell to attention as a rider strode past and reached the front of the army.

Alexander himself, their king, rode out in front of them, his helmet held at his side so everyone could see his face. He was a young man, younger than most people would probably expect him to be, but his soldiers knew that his youth was not a detriment at all to his abilities. In fact, it was comforting to think that he still might have so many years to keep leading them toward further victories, much longer than many generals could potentially have. He was not some child. There was wisdom and genius inside of that mind, a knowledge that was far greater than his age.

Alexander liked to be part of the battle, to be leading his armies from the front instead of from atop some nearby hill like many commanders did. Some of his inner circle thought that it was too dangerous for him to continue to do that as his campaign grew more and more vast. He had enemies all over the known world, so perhaps they were right, but Alexander wouldn't hear of it. He continued to be adamant that he was going to continue to guide his men toward victory personally, where they could see his face and he could see theirs. It helped bind them together, to feel like they knew him as they held the spears that he used to such devastating effect.

Alexander always looked brilliant as his horse paced before the rows of his armies. The king glanced up at the tall spears reaching up toward the clouds and smiled at the sight of them before his gaze dropped to the men holding those spears. Those were the people that he really treasured. He knew that those pikes in their hands were useless without warriors to wield them.

"My friends..." Alexander spoke loudly but softly. He had a soothing, comforting tone, but they had heard how quickly his words could become so powerful and fill them all with renewed vigor. "We continue in our hope and our belief that we are changing this world. And we are! I swear it! We already have changed so much! This is our destiny! Something that the gods themselves have given us! And we just have to accept it. That is all. If we can do that, then we can accomplish anything! We can show the gods and the rest of the world that we know how to wield this power and we know how to make all lands better lands! Are you with me!?"

Of course they were. The whole army roared with approval. Not a single soldier didn't believe in Alexander's cause. They all would follow him until the ends of the earth—and they were confident that he would bring them there.

Alexander's whole body seemed to shine with a miraculous glow, his fabled breastplate glistening with sunlight. There were some that said that it was his armor that was blessed by the gods, that was going to keep him safe and alive so that he could complete his work. His soldiers believed that. They had seen how the gods favored him and how he always found a way to survive the fight. He had to keep leading them. Without him, it would all fall apart. That armor would never fail him, not ever. It would ensure that Alexander of Macedon brought them all to the future he intended to build.

"You see?" Aegus asked, grinning. "We will make it through this. The future is ours!"

1

WORLD DOMINATION

Damon Meyer was nearing the age of thirty and hated every single second that brought him closer to that milestone. It was as if he could hear the final countdown ticking away toward the moment that he would be a failure, when he would lose any hope of being as great as he aspired to be. He had accomplished a lot in his twenty-eight years on the planet, but there was so much more that he wanted to do, so much more that he *could* do. He just needed to stay focused and never give up on the future that he had so carefully structured for himself.

Being one of the Visionaries was an honor but not always the easiest thing. Their group was undefined and unknown to most people in the world. They were a clandestine group of individuals that had a great deal of influence over the world's events, people that actually had a chance to make real change when most people could never actually hope to make any real difference in their lives. Still, they were not the closest group of people and rarely ever saw each other in person.

What the Visionaries did share was a dream to make a future that they could control, that would make the world a better place for generations to come. They all wanted that, and despite their conflicting ideas on a lot of other things, that dream kept them anchored to something that they could believe in.

Damon Meyer reached his computer and logged in to the chat room that he and the other Visionaries always used to communicate. None of them would dare risk all being gathered at once, so being together online would have to do. Thanks to one of the other Visionaries' technological prowess, they knew that their conversations were encrypted and hidden from any potentially prying eyes— except for the occasional blunder like what happened between David Purdue and Eve Wayneright.

They all had to just sit there back then after that billionaire artifact collector dared to threaten all of them after using Eve's computer. Eve died minutes later, having committed suicide to keep from divulging the Visionaries' secrets. She at least was loyal enough to kill herself before exposing them.

Since that unfortunate incident, their meetings had gone smoothly as they continued to orchestrate the world to bend toward how they wanted it to be. They were still in the middle of phase one of their plans of conquering the mindset of the world—destroying the relics and histories of the world to free people from the obsession with the past.

It was not the easiest thing to accomplish, he had to admit, but it was crucial to what they had planned. They wanted to save people from being stuck in the past and being held back by the histories that no longer should matter. The whole world, if they really wanted to make change, needed to focus on the future and the best way to reach tomorrow was to forget about what happened yesterday; at least, that was the philosophy.

Damon had been born into wealth but never knew what to really do with it. He didn't want to waste it all on some of the things that others in his situation would do. He stayed away from the temptations that wealth could push someone to fall into; he didn't touch any drugs, any expensive women, or any fancy cars. He had stayed focused his whole life on trying to do something great. He wanted to be something before he eventually died.

The Visionaries had found him and welcomed him into the formation of the group. They appreciated his donations and the things that his wealth helped to provide them, but he knew enough about them to know that he was not the only wealthy individual involved. He had sussed out that he was the youngest member of the Visionaries, though, and sometimes that shone through in their conversations. Some of them were too narrow-minded, and he did everything he could to help modernize their viewpoints, to expand their horizons.

Damon watched as the screen lit up and the other Visionaries logged in, though their faces were hidden behind their profiles, just as they always were. It was what kept them safe from people like David Purdue, that would have seen their faces otherwise. Ever since that encounter, they had been even more careful about keeping their identities hidden.

Many of the Visionaries did not even dare to speak anymore over the microphone. They preferred to type instead of talk to help even further protect themselves. Damon thought that was overboard and irritating but could understand why they might have preferred that route. They all wanted to keep themselves very safe. Damon thought that some of them were too cowardly, too afraid to make the big moves that he wanted to make.

Is everyone here?

"I am," Damon said. "Present and accounted for."

The others acknowledged their presence.

We must discuss our next actions. Burning down souvenir shops is not big enough. Our message is not as widespread as it should be. They are being treated as simple arsons, not as statements to the people of the world.

"I told you that would happen," Damon said with a shrug, leaning back in his chair. "We can worry about scrubbing the world clean of that kind of junk later. It's too small a scale for what we want to do right now. We need to do something large, something to make a real statement."

And what would you suggest then?

"I am going to hold off on getting into the specifics because none of my ideas matter while there is such a high risk to our plans right now."

What high risk are you talking about?

"Isn't it obvious?" Damon asked with a little laugh. He made sure that they could all hear how ridiculous he thought the question was. "David Purdue. The Order of the Black Sun. Doesn't any of that ring a bell? Let's be honest, the whole reason that we were stooping so low as to set fire to antique shops was because we were too rattled by his threats. We didn't want to do anything that would draw his attention...but those arsons did get his attention anyway, so it was all for nothing. We pointlessly held ourselves back. We should never be held back. We are supposed to be constantly moving toward the future, remember?"

There was a delay in a typed response. They must have been thinking about what they wanted to say. He wished that he could hear the silence that was no doubt on the other end of the call. They all knew that he was right. He had told them all that this exact scenario would happen, but they had all been too cautious—too scared, really—to do anything that was really worth their time. Finally, one of his fellow Visionaries sent a response.

It would be wiser to just stay clear of David Purdue and the Order of the Black Sun. They do not know what our plans are and they will not know if we just keep away from them. They have no way of finding us unless we do something that gives ourselves away. We avoid them and they will not trouble us.

Damon laughed again, even more loudly, to ensure that they heard. "You really think that that is the best move? You really think that's wise? What about that is wise? It sounds more like a cowardly thing to do to me. And given what they have done so far, I get the feeling that they would still find us even if we were doing everything we could to avoid them. David Purdue has proven to be relentless."

Which is exactly why we should not interact with him.

"We all heard him when he threatened us. He shouted at all of us, pointed right at the camera, and decided to tell us that he would be coming for us. You really think that a man like that isn't going to do everything he can to at least follow through with that?"

No one typed anything, and he knew that he finally had the proverbial floor. They were all his audience now, all realizing that he was making the most sense. They wanted to hear what he had to say, and he was happy to tell them what was on his mind.

"Before we move forward with any of our other plans, our primary objective should be to get rid of the threat that David Purdue and that secret society of his pose to us. The Order of the Black Sun's mission is in direct conflict with our own. They want to protect the past, and we want to shatter it so we can move on. We are diametrically opposed and nothing can change that. Nothing. And that's why we need to deal with them now instead of later. We are naturally going to continue to be at odds. We should preemptively get rid of that threat now."

How do you suggest we do that?

"I had something in mind," Damon said, rubbing his hands together. "In our research, we've learned a great deal about the members of the Order of the Black Sun. There is plenty that we can use. While I enjoy destroying history as much as the rest of you, we can sometimes use it as a weapon. We can take their past and turn it on them, sow distrust and descent, and then cripple them. When they are broken, we have them brought to us and we deal with them personally. We ensure that they can never bother us again."

No more words came on the screen for a few minutes again. They all must have been mulling over his proposal. He thought that the choice was obvious, but unfortunately, his colleagues did not always see the obvious scenario; they too often overcomplicated things. He was giving them vengeance on a silver platter and they were still apparently hesitant.

Finally, they responded.

We will move forward with your plan. Please tell us the specifics.

Damon grinned and barely held in his excitement. "Oh, there are a lot of specifics. The Order of the Black Sun loves the past so much...so I would like to see what happens when they are forced to face it."

2

THE THREE THIEVES

The Third Triumvirate was gone. Things had been quiet at the Musei Capitolini since those thieves disappeared. At first, everyone at the museum was on edge that those masked individuals could show back up and start trying to steal things again, but so far, there had not been any sign. They might have retired or been killed, or maybe they just realized that there was no point in stealing artifacts from thousands of years ago.

There had been rumblings that they were doing it for some kind of movement, some strange attempt to bring back the Roman Empire, but no one knew for certain, especially not Elio, who had only started as a guard for the museum in the past month or so. The night shift was serene and quiet and he really felt like he had nothing to worry about—at least, that was how he felt until that night.

It all started when he was doing his usual patrol down the corridors and wings of the museum. The lights were always off at night and he just had the flashlight in his hand to guide him and help him in his inspections. He would make sure that he did a thorough sweep of the building, taking extra care to check any of the dark corners or potential blind spots where some fool might try to hide and spend the night inside of the museum. He had been warned about such things happening and wanted to make sure it didn't happen on his watch. He needed a job, and he finally had one, so he had no intention of doing anything that might make him lose it.

Right when he was nearing the end of his check on the exhibit pertaining to Marcus Aurelius, he saw something out of the corner of his eye. He could have sworn that he had seen movement, but he was the only thing inside the museum that should have been moving at all. He swung his body around, wielding his flashlight to try and illuminate whatever had moved in the darkness. Thankfully, the spot where he thought he might find something was empty. There was nothing but the corner of the room.

He breathed a sigh of relief. It was so late, late enough that his mind must have just been playing tricks on him.

Then he heard a laugh and knew that it wasn't just his imagination. When he shined his light in the direction of the laughter, he found a silhouette standing on the other side of the room. The figure stood still and its face was covered by a mask that showed nothing but a frozen, passive expression. He recognized the face as one that he

The Guardians of lost time

had seen on a statue. The lips of the intruder's visage remained firmly closed as more laughter came from behind the mask.

"You think this is funny?" Elio called out. "You need to leave here immediately! You are trespassing!"

Elio tried to stop his hand from shaking. When he took the job as a security guard, he knew that there was a chance that something like this might happen. It was just a part of the job description, but he didn't expect to actually be face-to-face with someone that had broken into the museum. Still, no matter how frightened he was, he needed to do his job, and that meant that he needed to toss that person out of his museum and have them arrested. He mustered all of his courage and stomped over to the masked individual, trying to look as intimidating as possible. It didn't seem to have much effect, but it was hard to tell since he could not see the person's face.

"Are you deaf? I said you need to leave! Right now! The police are already on their way!"

The figure just stood perfectly still, looking determined to stay planted where they were. It was as if they were daring Elio to come get them, like they thought that he wouldn't stand a chance. They shouldn't have been so confident. Even if he didn't expect much action at that job, he still knew how to handle himself in a fight thanks to his own life experiences. They were in for a world of hurt if he got his hands on them. They didn't budge, and he was ready to throw that figure out onto the curb.

Suddenly, something hit him from his left and he stumbled to the floor. When he looked up, he saw another figure wearing a similar mask over their face. They put their pointer finger up to the frozen lip of the mask's face, warning him to be quiet. He had no intention of listening to them, though, even if he was outnumbered.

"You both need to get the hell out! Do you have any idea where you are and what you are doing!? This is a serious crime that you are committing! There will be severe punishment for this!"

"It's nothing that we haven't done before," a voice said, and it didn't sound like it was coming from either of the masked figures in front of him. He turned around and saw another masked intruder approaching. Unlike the first two, who looked like they were built like strong men, this one looked like a petite woman, and long curtains of black hair were draped down on either side of her mask, reaching down to her shoulders. "And you should not stand in our way. You will only get hurt."

As he looked at the three masked interlopers, he suddenly realized who they were. The stories about all of those museum robberies by three people wearing masks that resembled Ancient Roman emperors...that was exactly what he was looking at. There was no doubt in his mind that he was staring at that trio of famed thieves that must have just been dormant, waiting for their next chance to strike.

"You are the Third Triumvirate, aren't you?"

That must have made them smile but it was impossible to tell behind those passive stony lips on their masks.

They didn't respond, but he was already certain of the answer.

"Of course you are," Elio said, climbing to his feet. "So what is your plan now that you are back? Are you just going to start taking ancient artifacts again? Are you going to keep trying to bring back the Roman Empire and all of that? I heard people talk about that for months and everyone was in agreement that you all were crazy."

"No," the woman said. "We have no intention of doing that. Our ways have changed. We don't just take and preserve those old useless relics now. We don't need them for anything. No, now we just destroy them."

That was surprising to hear. From everything he had ever heard about the Third Triumvirate, it had sounded like they were obsessed with preserving and restoring the old ways. They had never gone out of their way to try to get rid of it before. It sounded unlike them but there was no doubt in his mind that he was looking at the same trio that had caused his country so much trouble before.

"Why destroy them?"

"The past needs to be purged, burned away, and forgotten for society to move on."

"You all have some epiphany in your time off? That's very different from what you used to preach."

"Things change. People evolve. That's what happens when you are no longer weighed down by the past. Now, you will let us do what we came here to do, and we will allow you to keep your life. It is quite simple."

"I can't let that happen."

Elio was going to prove his worth to the museum and to himself. His job was to protect the contents of that place and he was going to do that with every ounce of energy that he had. He wasn't going to let a few lunatics ruin a good thing. If anything, they were going to be proof that he had chosen the right career path.

"Alright then. Your choice is made."

Suddenly, all three of those masked figures were upon him. No matter how good his intentions were or how determined he was to fight, it didn't change that he was vastly outnumbered and completely overwhelmed by them. Even some of the best-trained fighters in the world probably wouldn't have stood a chance once the three of them converged on him.

As they beat him down, he knew that he wouldn't be able to protect the things that he was supposed to. He wouldn't be able to do his job to the best of his ability. He would be lucky if he even walked away with his life.

The one thing certain was that the Third Triumvirate was back—and worse than ever.

3

THE CURATOR'S LIST

Elijah Dane was not always the easiest person to talk to, but David Purdue had gotten used to the curator's judgmental and pessimistic views. He was accustomed to how little Elijah cared about people's feelings, taking far more stock in the artifacts that he inspected instead.

This was one of those moments as Purdue handed over his latest item to be stored away in the deep vault.

Elijah paid him as little mind as usual as he looked it over. It was a letter from the 1600s but was hardly anything special, at least compared to most of the things that they had managed to find and collect. Elijah even seemed less enthused by what was brought to him when usually he could be interested in most old things.

"This is underwhelming," Elijah said, glancing up at him from behind his glasses. "I expected more from the fearless leader of the Order of the Black Sun."

"Co-leader now, aye," Purdue reminded him. "And not everything we find is going to be impressive."

"Hmm," Elijah said in apparent agreement. "Evidently not. Let me tell you something, Purdue...a well-kept secret of mine."

Purdue's find must have been really boring for Elijah to open up that way. Usually he didn't make nearly as much conversation and definitely didn't usually share secrets of his.

"I have something of a personal wish list. There are things that I would absolutely love for one of you to bring here to me. Things that I would love to have a chance to see with my own eyes. It's been my hope to see some of those things come through that vault door, but unfortunately...that hasn't been the case. At least not yet."

Purdue didn't really care about the curator's list of things he wanted to see, but he decided to humor him and his hopes. "Go on then. What are some of the things you want to see? Maybe we can make it happen. I can't promise you that we can, but I'm willing to give it a try, aye?"

Elijah seemed to consider it for a long moment. It had to be tempting to have someone offer to make your dreams a reality. The truth was, if the curator's wish list was as challenging as he made it sound, it might be exactly what the Order of the Black Sun needed.

They had been so busy trying to find their mysterious new enemies but their foes were good at hiding. They needed a big win, at least as a distraction.

"Come on," Purdue cooed, putting his palms together to give a joking plea. "Just give me one of the things on this fabled wish list of yours, and I will do everything within my power to see that we get our hands on it and you can inspect it to your heart's content."

Purdue knew his own strengths. He knew that he could be persuasive, or at the very least, he could annoy someone enough until they gave in to his demands.

Elijah seemed like he wanted to withhold his hopes, like he was just relishing the fact that Purdue couldn't guess or couldn't read his mind, but he relented and offered one item from the list that he was talking about.

"Have you heard of Alexander the Great?"

"Of course I've heard of him," Purdue said. "He wouldn't be so great if he wasn't one of the most famous people on the planet, now would he?"

"I suppose not," Elijah said. He seemed a little surprised that Purdue had heard of him. He really must have thought he was an ignorant idiot that had no idea what he was doing. "Well, there has always been a legend that has intrigued me about him and his burial place."

"Didn't someone supposedly find his tomb a year or so ago?" Purdue could have sworn that he had heard about that.

"That has yet to be confirmed..." Elijah said with a touch of bitterness. He undoubtedly wanted to be the one to have gotten to inspect it. He always hated when other people curated important things since he didn't trust other people to do as thorough and careful of a job as he always did. "But it is not Alexander's resting place itself that captured my imagination. You see, according to old stories, Alexander's burial place was visited by Roman emperors, many of whom were inspired by the man and his many accomplishments, especially his talent for conquest. Augustus went there, for instance, but he was far from the only one. Even the worst of them still paid homage to the victories and the life of Alexander the Great. I'm sure you must have heard of Caligula."

"Aye," Purdue said. "One of the worst of the worst. A real depraved and crazy bastard that should never have been put into a position of power."

"That's him," Elijah said, once again acting impressed that Purdue knew anything at all. "Yes, even he went to Alexander's gravesite, but he didn't go there to pay respect. He went there because, like everything else, Caligula thought that he could just take whatever he wanted."

"He took something from the grave?"

"Oh, yes," Elijah said, his eyes glinting with excitement. "A piece from Alexander's armor that he was buried in. The breastplate, to be precise."

"Why?"

"Why not? It's hard to know with a man like Caligula. He did all kinds of things that would not have made sense to most people. There were not always logical or reasonable explanations for why he did the things that he did. But...if I had to take a guess, it might have had something to do with the stories surrounding Alexander's breastplate. The soldiers that fought for him claimed that the breastplate protected Alexander from any harm on the battlefield."

"And you believe that?"

"I would like to, and considering how many things we have here in this very room that have similar properties, it is not outside the realm of possibilities. The only way to know for certain if there is any validity to those stories would be to get a closer look at them. Which is exactly why—"

"Which is why you want me to find it, aye. I get it."

Elijah stared at him from behind those glasses. "Don't tell me you're not interested in it. It's better than eighty percent of the garbage that you and the rest of the order have been bringing me lately. What I am giving you here is gold...well, better than gold, actually. Far better."

"I'm interested," Purdue said honestly. "I'm just trying to think about who would be best to bring along on this expedition. Considering how passionate you are and that you are the one that brought this to my attention to begin with…you should come with us to find Alexander's breastplate."

Elijah didn't look enthused. They both knew that field missions were not his favorite thing to do. He would much rather be sitting around in the Order of the Black Sun compound, looking over all of the priceless artifacts that he protected. He preferred to be the one that people brought their findings to rather than the one that went out and found anything. That was just the kind of person he was—but exceptions had been made in the past.

"Come on," Purdue prodded. "You are really telling me that you don't want to be the one to find something on your sacred wish list? If you are so annoyed that none of us have brought any of those things to you yet, then you might just have to do it yourself."

"You might have a point," Elijah said.

Purdue was pleased by his own continued persuasiveness. He just had a way of bending people to his will sometimes. He really did want the curator to be part of it, though. He obviously had passion, and in his experience, passion was what could lead to success. It always made the search much stronger to have someone that really cared about the subject matter.

"Fine," Elijah said. "It's hard to resist the possibility of actually getting my hands on it early. Besides, I don't want you and all of the ones out there like you scratching it or anything. I will at least be sure that it is handled with care."

"That's the spirit. Let me put a team together. I'll consult with Nina and let you know."

Elijah adjusted his glasses. "Just promise me that you won't pick any of the insufferable ones."

Purdue laughed. "I'll do my best."

∽

THE IMPERIAL THIEF

Gaius knew better than to question the commands of the emperor. Everyone in Rome knew that the emperor's word was law and that to disobey him was treachery. Nothing good would come from rejecting what the emperor said; his word was always absolute—especially Caligula's.

Caligula was different from the emperors that came before him. Every Roman citizen could see that, especially after all of the peculiar things he had done that made many suspect that he had succumbed to madness. Nobody dared to speak those thoughts aloud, however, or they would certainly lose their tongues—or worse. The people that worked for the emperor knew that his depraved imagination had no limits. If you crossed him, a quick death would be a blessing.

Still, Gaius was not sure that he heard Caligula correctly when the emperor turned to him and gave him a command.

"Dig him up. Now."

That could not have been right. He must have misheard what he said as Caligula stood with a small contingent of followers at the burial site of the legendary ruler, Alexander the Great. Surely Caligula would not defile the grave of such a revered and prodigious figure.

Gaius hesitated, glancing at everyone else around him, who all averted their gazes. They were all used to odd requests from their emperor, but this one seemed particularly strange. They all must have just been relieved that Caligula wasn't talking to them.

"I'm sorry, sir..." Gaius said carefully, trying not to upset the mad emperor. "Might I have misheard you? You wish for me to dig up Alexander's remains?"

"Your ears seem to be working properly," Caligula said, his beady eyes narrowing. "Now do as I say and show me what's left of Alexander. Do it quickly or I will find someone that will."

That wasn't an empty threat. Caligula would have him killed on a whim for some minor infraction, including taking too long. The emperor was an impatient man who did not enjoy having his precious time wasted by anyone, let alone his underlings. Gaius couldn't wait any longer, no matter what reservations he had. He didn't want to join Alexander in death.

Gaius quickly fumbled for a spade and started to dig. It would have been faster if others were helping him exhume the remains, but no one assisted his efforts. Caligula probably wanted it that way, to teach him a lesson for even hesitating. Gaius tried not to show how difficult it was. He didn't want to give Caligula any satisfaction as the emperor watched him dig.

As he dug deeper into the earth, Caligula crouched down so that he could address him more closely—still above him, of course. "You are going to find me whatever is left of Alexander. His breastplate was buried with him. You are going to retrieve it for me."

Gaius had never been a thief, but now the emperor of Rome himself was commanding him to become one. If that was what he was bid to do by someone like that, then that was exactly what he had to become. He had no real choice in the matter. It just had to be done.

"I am going to ask you a question, servant, and you must answer me honestly." Caligula didn't even bother to address Gaius by his name. He probably didn't know it. The way he spoke was always so domineering. He did not request things or ask things of others. He simply told them what to do, knowing that they would have to obey. "Do you believe that Alexander was as great as the stories say?"

Gaius had never thought much about that before. "I am not sure."

"How are you not sure of your own opinion?" Caligula snorted. "Was he or wasn't he? From your probably skewed perspective, of course. I am curious to know how the lesser citizens of my empire view the man."

"I suppose he was then."

"Why?"

Gaius hated being interrogated like that but there was no way that he could make it stop. "Because others who know better than I have said as much."

"Ah, I see," Caligula said. "So your intelligence is based solely on what others tell you to believe. Do you not have any thoughts or insights of your own?"

The emperor was goading him, that much was obvious. He seemed to enjoy poking at Gaius like he was trying to antagonize him enough for him to break, and then he would punish him for his insolence.

"It is probably better that way. If people as lowly as yourself believed that they actually knew about things that were so far above them, things would probably become very upended. We don't need your kind to actually have opinions. We just need you to do as we say. And by we, I mean me. Now keep digging and don't stop until Alexander's remains are found."

Gaius did as was commanded and kept stabbing into the dirt over and over. He wasn't given any assistance and was constantly being nagged by Caligula. He just had to endure it, though, and just hope that eventually he would find something in the earth and be done with the whole affair.

Finally, he felt his spade make contact with something. He looked down at where he had blunged the tool; Caligula had obviously heard the sound too. He flashed a broad smile and got to his feet, looking down into the hole.

"What are you waiting for, you fool? Keep going. Get it out of there."

The emperor could say whatever he wanted, no matter how much it bothered his subject. He could call him by any name or by any insult, it didn't matter. Nothing could be done except to follow his instructions to the letter.

Gaius kept digging and trying to get a better grip on whatever was in that hole. He didn't want to disturb the body of Alexander the Great, but he did not have much choice in the matter. If he didn't do it, the emperor would have his head along with whatever was left of the Macedonian king.

After shaking off some more dirt, Gaius found himself looking down at a piece of armor and the bones of the one that once wore it. He was staring at the remains of one of the most famous men in history and the breastplate that he was buried in—the one that was supposed to be able to protect the person wearing it from harm. He must not have been wearing it when he died.

Caligula was looking over his shoulder. "Is that it then? Pull it up! Pull it up!"

The emperor was manic, nearly jumping up and down with giddiness when he watched Gaius pull the breastplate off of the bones of Alexander and bring it out of the hole.

"Give it to me! Give it to me now!"

Caligula snatched the armor out of Gaius's hands and admired it on his own. "Yes...this is it. The greatest armor that has ever been made blessed by the gods themselves to protect the one that wears it. No one would be able to harm me when I have this on."

There were many peculiarities to the emperor, but one of the most pronounced was his paranoia. He always thought that people were conspiring against him, wishing him harm. Maybe he was right, considering how many people disliked him or were scared of him. Gaius wouldn't be surprised if someone tried to eliminate him, so maybe he was smart to preemptively find things that might protect him from an assassination.

The breastplate of Alexander the Great might be exactly what he needed.

4

THE RETURN OF THE TRIUMVIRATE

Purdue went straight to Dr. Nina Gould's office in the compound. She was the biggest lover of history that he knew. She would probably want to hear all about it and maybe want to come along on the search itself if he was lucky. They always worked well together.

When he found her, though, she didn't even notice him at first. She was staring at the pages inside an open folder. Whatever she was looking at must have been enthralling for her not to hear him come inside the room. When he took another step, the floor creaked and her head sprang up. She looked surprised to see him but then nodded to herself.

"Purdue. There's something you have to see." Nina looked grave—no, even worse than that; she looked livid. But as he approached her, he could see that he was not the target of her ire. Instead, her anger stemmed from the folder on her desk that she slid across the table to him. "Just look."

Purdue did as he was asked and opened it up. The folder was full of photographs printed out. From the looks of them and the time stamp coding in the corner, they looked like images captured from a security camera.

The first picture he looked at showed a broken glass door and three figures stepping through the shattered opening. At first glance, he didn't notice anything out of the ordinary besides the apparent crime being committed. But then he pulled out the second picture, which showed a clearer image of the ones that were breaking through that door—and showed their faces.

Each of the criminals shared passive, stony expressions because they all wore familiar-looking masks. Each mask was in the molding of a face, like a statue. Purdue recognized those masks immediately. Those were the visages of three ancient individuals like they had been plucked right off a bust at a museum. They looked just like the masks that the criminal trio, the Third Triumvirate, used to wear.

That shouldn't have been possible. The Third Triumvirate was gone. Two of their members were dead, and the third—Callie—now worked with them and made up for her past sins as a member of the Order of the Black Sun.

"When was this taken?" It had to be an old picture from a crime that happened back then.

"A week ago in Sicily," Nina said, biting a nail nervously. She looked like she was a ticking time bomb about to explode. "The Third Triumvirate still exists. We were stupid to trust her...to take her in." She was obviously referring to Callie.

"That can't be right," Purdue said. He wasn't convinced. "Callie wouldn't have done this, and the other two...they are dead!"

"So *she* said," Nina said, crossing her arms. "But I didn't see any bodies. Did you? We just took her word for it."

"Why, though? It wouldn't make sense. Callie has spent so long trying to redeem herself. She's done everything to try to earn our trust."

"Exactly," Nina said. "Getting us to trust her so she can stab us in the back."

"We shouldn't jump to those kinds of conclusions."

"We're not jumping to anything!" Nina said, pressing her finger down on the pictures in front of them, pointing right at the woman with the long dark hair wearing that mask—the woman that looked so much like Callie. "This seems pretty evident."

"It's suspicious and cause for some concern, aye...but we should at least talk to her about it and see what she says. I assume you haven't spoken to her?"

"Of course not," Nina said. "I would probably end up strangling her if I did."

"Then it's best that I talk to her then."

Of course Nina was feeling betrayed, considering how violent her relationship with Callie had been when they first met and how long it took for her to trust her. To have all of that have been a lie, to have fallen for some kind of ruse...it was understandably infuriating.

"She still hasn't even told us her real name, Purdue," Nina said. "She's practically been going around still calling herself Miss Caligula."

"I'll talk to her," Purdue said sternly. "I will, aye? Right now. But you have to promise me that you are not going to do anything until I have had the chance to talk to her. At least give me that chance to try to get to the bottom of all of this."

Nina didn't seem thrilled by the idea, but luckily, she still trusted him. "Fine. But you tell me what she says immediately."

Purdue trusted his gut instinct. He glanced back down at the pictures, putting them back in the folder and tucking it under his arm. Before he left the room, he turned back to his longtime colleague.

"I really don't believe this was her."

Nina sighed. "We'll see."

If the breastplate of Alexander involved one of the Roman emperors, then he knew exactly who to go to. There was only one person in the Order of the Black Sun that had the credentials that he was looking for, that knew enough about Caligula to possibly be able to really lend him the kind of assistance that he needed—Callie, the woman that used to use that emperor's name when she used to steal Roman artifacts.

When she was Miss Caligula and wore a mask that replicated the stone face of her namesake, she worked with two others in the infamous Third Triumvirate. Their mission was to restore the Ancient Roman Empire to its former glory, hoping that protecting the relics of that time could help inspire others to join their mission. It was an objectively foolhardy errand to try to do something like that, but they didn't seem to mind. Miss Caligula, Mr. Commodus, and Mr. Nero worked tirelessly to bring about their dream, but during a time when they tried to seek out the sword of Julius Caesar, they were beaten by Nina. That was when Miss Caligula became an enemy, but things had changed since then. Purdue was convinced that Miss Caligula had changed as well.

Since her other triumvirate friends had been executed and Callie joined forces with them against a common enemy, she had done all she could to try to redeem herself. It took some people longer to accept her than it did others, but Purdue was more than willing to give her a chance. So far, she hadn't let him down, so he usually had no trouble going to her for help.

Still, the story about those new masked individuals had unnerved him. It sure sounded like the old Third Triumvirate. He really hoped that she wasn't involved. Now he could at least gauge her reaction and hope for the best. He didn't want to suspect her or condemn her until he knew for sure, so he would have to tread carefully.

Callie sat in the compound's library, her attention completely enraptured by the book in front of her. She didn't even notice him enter the room at first.

"Somebody is doing some homework, aye?"

When Callie looked up, she brushed her long raven hair out of her eyes. She looked a little bit startled by the interruption and more than a little surprised that it was Purdue that had been the one to startle her.

"Purdue...hi." She closed the book to give him her attention, but Purdue couldn't help but glance at the hardcover in front of her. It was a textbook on Ancient Rome.

"Feeling nostalgic, are we?" Purdue asked carefully. He didn't want to upset her, but he couldn't help but prod a little bit. If she was innocent, his taunts wouldn't make much of a difference. "Are you looking back on the glory days?"

At first, she seemed confused by what he meant but then followed his gaze to the book. Her face grew red and she let out a little laugh. "Oh, yes. Well, just because I gave up on wanting to bring all of this back doesn't mean that all of it doesn't still fascinate me."

"Of course. Makes sense. That's actually why I wanted to talk to you," Purdue said. He needed to be wise with his words and how he delivered them. "I have enacted a new operation for the Order of the Black Sun. We are going to recover the breastplate of Alexander the Great. But already, in my research, I have hit something of a snag that I need help with. Your help, aye."

"What is this snag?" she asked knowingly. "Is it perhaps that Caligula took the breastplate from Alexander?"

Purdue shouldn't have been surprised. All he could do was chuckle and applaud her. "You're right about that, aye. You're good. It does seem that it was taken from him, and I'm not sure where he would have taken it from there. I figured that you would know best considering..."

"Considering that I wore Caligula's face over my own for some time? Is that what you mean?"

He knew to keep treading carefully, just in case. "Something like that. I just know that with your history, you are an expert on the subject."

"Are you trying to flatter me?"

"No, no, no. Not at all. What I'm trying to do is ask you to come on this next expedition with me. How would you like to be the one to help find what Caligula took? Hell, he might have even held the thing at one point. How can you pass up an opportunity like that?"

Callie's mouth curved into a surprise smile and her eyes started to swell up with liquid. She looked more than just surprised—she was moved by the invitation. Usually, she was just assigned to an operation. It was rare that someone sought her out for her expertise.

"Of course I will go with you!" she said, beaming. "You would be foolish to leave me behind on that one."

"Of course I would," Purdue said. "And we both know that I am no fool."

Now came the hard part, but it was essential to making sure that he could trust the people that he was working with. He started to speak, and her smile faded.

"There is something that I need to ask you if you are going to be working with me on this. I need to be able to rely on the people around me, especially under such dangerous circumstances. I need to know that I can trust you."

Callie looked disappointed. "I still haven't proven myself, have I? Even after everything I've done?"

"You have..." Purdue said honestly. "If not for some recent news, we would not have to have this conversation."

"What news?"

It was no use keeping the information from her anymore. He pulled out the folder that he was holding behind his back and showed her its contents. One by one, he let her look at the surveillance images. Callie didn't speak as she examined them all carefully, spending a good few minutes on each one. For the most part, her expression was hard to read. He did notice her give a slight shake of her head though as she looked over the photographs.

After a long while, she pulled her attention away from the photographs and brought it back up to him. "What the hell is this?"

"I was hoping you could tell me," Purdue said.

"You don't think that I actually had something to do with this, do you?" When he didn't answer her immediately, she rolled her eyes and clutched her trembling hands together. "That's why you were talking to me about trust...you really do think that I might have done this? You think one of these people is me?"

"I don't," Purdue said as calmly and as honestly as he could. "But you can't really fault me for making sure, aye? I mean, just look at them."

"I see them," she growled, not looking back down at the pictures. "Either this is an old picture of when the Third Triumvirate was still a thing, or someone is playing some kind of game."

"This was taken last week."

"Then, like I said, someone is playing a game. A copycat or something, I don't know. Obviously, this has nothing to do with me."

"I believe you," Purdue said firmly. "And I agree. Some sly bastards are putting on those masks to send a message. Or they might believe in the cause that you used to believe in..."

"So you don't just want my help because I know about Ancient Rome. You want me to help you with whatever this is. Or maybe you just want to keep a close eye on me."

Purdue wasn't sure of the real answer to that. It might have been a mixture of all three. All he knew was that, whichever it was, Callie was going to be an asset in what was ahead.

Callie still seemed frustrated but bit back on her anger. She even formed a smile. "I guess you'll just have to see for yourself. Thanks for including me."

5

QUESTIONS AND SUSPICIONS

Sam Cleave was not pleased about being left behind. He hated having to stay back and babysit the other members of the secret society. That was one of his least favorite things in the world. He was pissed off when Purdue explained to him that staying back was exactly what he was going to have to do.

However, he was even angrier when Purdue started to just calmly question him about Callie and her potential intentions. He even showed Sam the pictures just to give him a visual and to show him that this wasn't everyone being paranoid. They possibly had a real reason to be concerned. Sam did not want to hear any of it, though. He looked at one of the pictures for five seconds before scoffing and handing it back.

"It's not her," Sam said bluntly after hardly even examining it. "That's not her at all."

"How can you be so sure?" Purdue asked. "Maybe she wasn't able to stay on the straight and narrow after retiring from the whole thieving business, aye? Who is to say that she hasn't fallen off the rails again?"

"I am here to say that," Sam said. "No. Callie left all of that behind a while ago. She knows better than to go back to that part of her life, and she obviously would know that we would find out immediately after she did it. She's not stupid, Purdue."

"You don't think that we should keep all potential possibilities open?"

"Not when the answer is already obvious," Sam said, folding his arms. "I really hope that you all didn't already accuse her of this."

Purdue snickered uncomfortably. "Well...it wasn't so much an accusation...but I did have to ask her about it. I showed her the pictures and—"

"And made her feel like she was being interrogated and mistrusted, I'm sure," Sam said sharply, interrupting Purdue. "Jesus Christ. You all sure know how to make a little mess into a big one. How quickly everyone immediately forgets all of the good she did. It's like you all were waiting for some kind of reason to turn your back on her again."

"That's not fair," Nina said, standing in the doorway. She walked in, looking livid. "Why are you acting like we are crazy for even considering the possibility that she might have been playing us this whole time? She *was* a criminal before. There is precedence for this, Sam."

"You said it yourself. She *was* a criminal. She isn't anymore. I know that for a fact. She would have had nothing to do with whatever the hell is going on in those pictures. I can guarantee that."

"I'm not going to risk the safety and security of the order because you make a guarantee."

"There is nothing at risk," Sam said. He was getting heated, his face growing red. "She isn't a danger to any of us. She has helped us on a lot of expeditions now! And before that, she saved me from those bastards torturing me. You guys couldn't even do that." Sam slammed his hand on his table. "For Christ's sake, Callie is the only reason that I'm here!"

For a moment, that point seemed to silence Nina. Purdue certainly started to question himself when things were put in that perspective. There really wasn't anyone in the Order of the Black Sun that knew Callie better than Sam. He was the one that would be able to tell if she was a traitor or a spy. He was defending her with so much passion; he obviously believed that she had been reformed.

Nina spoke calmly but still didn't back down. "She saved you. Yes. We all will always be grateful for that, but she is going to remain a suspect until it is proven otherwise. We would be foolish to let our guards down around her."

Sam folded his arms. "I'll keep an eye on her here then while you're off looking for that armor."

"We are taking her with us," Purdue said. "Caligula might have been involved in the breastplate being lost to begin with. There is no one that knows more about Caligula here than Callie. She would be useful."

"Make whatever excuse you want," Sam said. "Let's be honest. You are only dragging her along with you so you can keep an eye on her yourselves. And if she does betray you, you can be the ones to put her down, is that it?"

"It's not like that," Purdue said. "Really. I don't think it's her. I really don't. But we need to be cautious in these kinds of situations."

"Yeah, whatever," Sam said. "You don't have to trust her, but I would like to think that you would trust me by this point. I know for a fact that she would not go back to that life. And the fact that I'm the one telling you that should give you enough of a reason to cut all this paranoia crap. She's one of us now. She has been for a while. Go on and find that armor. I'm sure at some point, you'll see how wrong you both were to doubt her—and to doubt me.."

It wasn't the best place to leave a conversation, but Purdue knew that any further discussion would just ramp up the tension again. He needed his friends to all be on the same page, but that wasn't possible, so if he couldn't have them be on the same page, he could at least try to make sure that they all stayed on the same book.

"Good luck out there," Sam said half-heartedly. "And if you ever find yourself in a tough bind, believe me, that girl will get you out of it."

∽

The flight in the private jet toward Italy was very uncomfortable. Despite the group being composed of people that Purdue enjoyed working with, the new developments with the masked thieves had unnerved everyone. All of the old suspicions and skepticism that Nina and Elijah had toward Callie had returned with a vengeance. Purdue wished that they wouldn't rush to conclusions, but he also couldn't blame them after everything she had put them through when she had been Miss Caligula.

The conversation with Sam before they left, though, kept echoing in his brain. Sam was so sure about her, so why was it so hard for everyone else to trust her too?

Elijah came over and sat beside him, speaking quietly so that no one else on the aircraft could overhear them. He cleaned off his glasses as he spoke, and when he put them back on, he stared at Callie, who lay asleep in her seat. The curator stared at her curiously, like he was nervous that she would suddenly wake up to attack him.

"I have been brought up to speed on the current Miss Caligula situation..." Elijah kept his voice very low but his whispers were full of concern. "Do you really think that it is wise to have her on this expedition...all things considered? I would have thought that you would want her to be locked in her room in the compound until we can prove her innocence or until she confesses."

"Her name is Callie now, not Miss Caligula," Purdue said sternly. "Don't forget that. As far as how I am dealing with it...yes, we need her on this assignment, considering how it could be connected to Caligula. She's an expert on that particular emperor."

"Because she wore his face during his crimes?" Elijah asked coldly. He really had no tact at all.

"That mask was of Caligula, aye, but she really does know a lot about him. More than Nina. More than me. And more than you. Don't tell me that you have already decided that she is guilty, Elijah. I thought you liked to get a thorough look at things before making up your mind about them."

"That is what I do with relics, yes, but it's a little bit different with people. I tend to expect the worst from them, so the idea that she never gave up that mask at all and is still a thief...that sounds entirely possible, if not probable. We can't all be as forgiving as you, Purdue."

"I'm tired of arguing with people about this," Purdue said. He really was so sick of having to defend her and defend his decision to bring her. Whether it was Nina waving those pictures in his face, Elijah upset that they were suspecting Callie, and now Elijah already giving up on her, it was infuriating to have to keep fighting about it. Purdue was taking a very neutral ground. As far as he was concerned, Callie was innocent until she was proven to be guilty; it wasn't the other way around. "She's on this assignment. She's here to stay. That's all there is to it. The only way that changes is if she does turn out to be back to her old ways."

"And if that happens?" Elijah asked. "What would we do then?"

"Whatever we have to."

He meant that, but he still had hope that it wouldn't come to that.

∼

Before starting their quest to find the breastplate of Alexander the Great, it was decided that they should try to clear up what was happening with the reemergence of the Third Triumvirate. Mainly, they all wanted an answer as to whether or not Callie was innocent or not and they wanted that answer sooner rather than later. It wasn't smart to take someone that they didn't trust on an assignment, so before they got too far, they needed to know if she could still be trusted.

The best way to do that was to speak with the one that had seen the Third Triumvirate recently with his own eyes. They went to the museum of the Third Triumvirate's latest hit and spoke to the one that had confronted them that night.

The security guard, Elio, looked like he had been thrown through a meat grinder. He had been beaten to a pulp, still bruised and bloody from the assault that he had been through at the museum. The Third Triumvirate—or whoever they were—had nearly put him in a coma with the beating that they gave him. The trio that they had encountered before were violent and dangerous, but this seemed somehow more brutal.

Purdue instinctively glanced over at Callie and tried to figure out what she thought as she looked at the man in the hospital bed. She looked mortified and sad, but he was really looking for some guilt, some kind of tell that she knew him or knew what had happened to him. However, she looked just as alarmed as everyone else in the room. He really didn't want her to be involved in any of this and hoped that this talk might clear some things up and hopefully clear her name as well.

However, when he turned to Nina, she was also watching Callie closely, and she looked like she was already condemning her for the actions that she claimed she had nothing to do with. It was a complex situation for everyone in that hospital room, and the tension was thick and palpable.

"I'm sorry this happened to you," Purdue said, taking the lead. "I really am. We were just hoping to ask you a few questions."

The security guard seemed agreeable and cooperative despite his injuries. He needed to share what he had been through, to try to really heal from the ordeal.

"It was them. The ones that stole from all of those exhibits. The Third Triumvirate. They were—"

"It wasn't them," Callie interrupted, glaring at the injured man. "It wasn't the Third Triumvirate. They don't exist anymore."

"I'm sorry, but that is who I saw. They had those masks... ones that looked like they came right off an old statue. It was them. I would know those anywhere. It was just like—"

"No!" Callie shouted, silencing the man.

Elio fell silent and Purdue slowly guided Callie away from him. "Excuse us for one moment."

When they were out of earshot, Purdue shook his head and swore under his breath. "I didn't bring you along so that you could scare witnesses into not talking to us. That's not a good look, aye?"

"I don't know what he saw, but—"

"He *told* us what he saw and whether you like what he's saying or not does not matter. What matters is letting him tell us whatever he knows, things that might be beneficial. If that's too hard for you to hear, then we can't have you around. I'll fly you right back to the compound if you can't pull yourself together."

That seemed to snap Callie out of it a little. She looked over at Elio with some shame, and then her expression became sullen. "I'm sorry. It's just...it's hard to hear people talk about it. They really believe that it's the Third Triumvirate...but it's not."

"We are going to figure all of that out, I promise. But having a meltdown and acting this way is just making you look more suspicious. It's not helping anything and definitely not helping our search, aye? You get that?"

Callie nodded.

Purdue still wasn't going to take the risk of having her around during the questioning, though. She had already proven that she could not keep her emotions in check when it came to the topic of the new Third Triumvirate.

When Purdue got back to Elio, he was busy talking to Nina and Elijah, doubling down on what he had said in front of Callie. "They were as real as you and me, and they were just like all of those pictures and videos. It was those thieves, alright. The very same. I don't doubt that."

Purdue hoped that he was wrong.

∼

Purdue tried to get them all to refocus on the armor that they were after instead of their suspicions about Callie. The interview with that security guard had been full of speculation and one man's opinion. It was hardly damning evidence. Until they had something like that, she was welcome to stay.

Unfortunately, Nina and Elijah were not as keen on moving on to a different topic of discussion.

"If we seek out the breastplate that Caligula stole, then this new Third Triumvirate might find its way to us, right?"

"I suppose..."

"So we wouldn't just be getting something incredible for the deep vault, we would also have a chance to figure out just what the hell we are dealing with here and why the Third Triumvirate has miraculously come back."

"They're not back," Callie said firmly, crossing her arms defiantly. "These are just imposters."

Purdue was inclined to believe her when she talked about the new Third Triumvirate. It didn't seem like she was just trying to cover her own tracks. The way that Nina and Elijah kept looking at her, though... It was obvious that they weren't as certain. They would need to see the faces behind those masks to really believe that she had nothing to do with it.

"You guys really don't believe me, do you?" Callie asked, mostly looking at Nina and Elijah. "You really think that I would go back to that life?"

Nina sighed, but it still looked like she was trying to see if the former thief was lying or not. "I don't want to believe that, but I have to keep all options open in my mind. There is precedence to believe that you might have put on a mask and stolen something, after all. I just don't want to be blindsided."

"Or you could just trust me," Callie snapped. "I thought I had proven myself to you all."

"You have," Purdue cut in. "You have, aye, and we are going to figure this out and clear your name. Simple as that."

"I shouldn't have to clear my name. I already did that."

Elijah, as usual, lacked any kind of tact or empathy in his own response. "All we are doing is looking at things objectively. You were once a member of the Third Triumvirate, the brains behind their operation no less, and now they are back and one of them looks conspicuously like yourself. You know me. I look at evidence. I look at what is presented to me. This is no different. Once I see that the evidence rules you out, then I will know for certain that you are not involved. That is just the way that it is. It is nothing personal."

"It feels personal," Callie hissed through gritted teeth.

She stomped off toward the rental car, obviously not wanting to hear any more of the conversation. Purdue couldn't blame her for being upset. It had to be hard to suddenly be regarded with so much suspicion after spending so long proving yourself to the same people that now were judging her.

Nina and Elijah watched her walk away and looked undeterred from their thoughts. It was like they thought at any moment she could run away and put on one of those statue-like masks that the Third Triumvirate liked to wear.

"You guys are going too hard on the girl," Purdue said.

"No, we're not," Nina said. "You didn't fight her like I did back then. You don't know what she's capable of."

"I heard the stories, and I still had to face the Third Triumvirate once or twice."

"It's not the same," Nina said. "She tried to kill me in the Coliseum."

"I remember, aye," Purdue said. "I get it. But if she is innocent, then all of this interrogation is only going to have made a rift with one of our own. Don't you see that?"

Elijah shrugged and wiped off his glasses. "We see it. But it's like we said. We can't cast aside any possibilities. We have to consider each carefully. The truth will become apparent eventually."

Purdue was so frustrated by the drama happening within the Order of the Black Sun. All of this confusion about the Third Triumvirate was just a distraction and one that was poisoning all of them against one another. They needed to stay united, especially when there was still a hidden enemy out there.

"What we should be doing is focusing on finding the breastplate of Alexander the Great, no? Isn't that what we are doing here?" Purdue was having trouble hiding his frustrations. It was hard when he was just so irritated with everyone's priorities. "Yes, it may lead to this new Third Triumvirate, but whether it does or not, this expedition was started in order to find that piece of armor. We are doing this to find something for you to check off of your wish list, Elijah. We can't forget that."

That seemed to snap the curator away from his preoccupation with the Third Triumvirate witch hunt. His fascination with the breastplate and his desire to find it and study it himself hopefully outweighed his desire to prove that Callie was somehow betraying them.

Elijah readjusted his glasses as if he was now starting to see clearly again and nodded. "You're right. We need to be thinking more about Alexander than we are Callie."

Hopefully that was enough to at least delay the inevitable explosion that was being fueled by the paranoia and tension. Although, he knew that he wouldn't be able to stop that for long. Eventually, they would need answers about who was now wearing those masks.

6

THE SEARCH FOR THE BREASTPLATE

Despite how much misplaced anxiety the two of them had, Purdue was glad to have Nina and Elijah with him on the expedition. Between Nina's extensive knowledge of history and Elijah's obvious passion for finding the breastplate, he had two people that knew a lot about what they were searching for to help fill him in on all of the details.

Alexander the Great was one of the most famous men in history, but there was still a lot that Purdue didn't know about him. He knew that he was a great conqueror and helped topple the Persian Empire. He knew that when he died, it caused a whole lot of civil wars among his surviving generals, that were all fighting over the power vacuum that he left behind. Outside of that, there was a lot that he still had to learn about what made Alexander so great.

"He was a military genius," Elijah said. "It was his tactics that won him so many battles, not necessarily his greater numbers. That, along with some innovative weaponry..." Of course, as usual, Elijah put a huge emphasis on the historical items used. That was always his focus. "The sarissa, for instance."

Elijah took out a notepad and drew a long spear as a crude diagram, even making notations showing how long the spear was to paint a better picture of it. The little scribbles said thirteen to twenty feet long.

"They were these incredibly long spears that his infantry used to devastating effect. Initially developed by Alexander's father, Phillip II, they weren't put to their best use until Alexander took the crown. They were part of what was called the Macedonian phalanx, which was also developed by Alexander's father, mind you. So often, the son just capitalizes on what the father created. That is just the way of life sometimes."

"That phalanx?" Purdue was sure that he had heard of that before, but he didn't exactly know much about it.

"It was a battle formation," Nina said. "Essentially made the best use of the sarissa by creating this wall of spears that held their enemies in place. It was highly effective and became a standard for many militaries until the Romans started to come up with arguably better maneuvers."

"It's not arguable," Callie said. "The Roman's formations were better. That's just evolution over time."

There was an awkward silence lingering for a moment. Callie giving any praise to Ancient Rome seemed to put Nina and Elijah on edge again, but Purdue spoke up, determined to break through the discomfort that plagued their group.

"That's impressive, all around, aye," Purdue said. "So these sarissa kept their enemies at an arm's length—or, much more than that, I should say. That's pretty smart. Your enemy's weapons aren't exactly useful if they can't reach you but you can still reach them."

"Exactly," Elijah said. "They were disastrous for his enemies and allowed him to sweep across so many other armies. This legion of pikes that could not be reached and would impale anyone that dared to get in their way."

"Alexander would have conquered so much more of the world if his army didn't lose morale," Nina said. "They had won so many battles and gone so far that many just needed a break. They were too far away from home and it was them that made him turn back and return to Macedon. Unfortunately, he never was able to go back out and conquer more after that. He died at home. He was only thirty-two years old when he died. Imagine what he could have accomplished had he lived longer. He would have done even more than he already had."

That was true. He did die relatively young, though not relatively young for the time. If he had decades more to continue to conquer and win, then he might have taken over the entirety of the world. Then the term "great" probably wouldn't be enough to do him justice.

"How did he die?" Purdue asked. He was trying to rack his brain to remember if he had ever heard it before. Typically with people like that throughout history, he imagined it was probably some kind of assassination. That was what usually befell leaders like him. "Who killed him?"

Nina snickered and rolled her eyes. She was used to Purdue not being as knowledgeable about the details of history as her, but it always amused her when he had such an obvious hole in his knowledge. "Who killed him? Typhoid or malaria."

That made both Nina and Elijah laugh. Purdue knew what they meant. Obviously he hadn't been killed by anyone and instead had died from some illness. That was also a pretty common way to go back in the old days when there was no real good medicine. It didn't take much for a sickness to end someone's life, even someone as powerful and as influential as Alexander, clearly.

"There are multiple different accounts of where Alexander was buried, and no one still knows with absolute certainty where that is. There is a more recent finding that seems like it could be promising, but even they have not fully confirmed with absolute certainty that it is him." Elijah talked about the body in terms of being a curator, with an obvious desire to have been the one to find and take care of the bones of one of the most famous men in history. "But the story has always been that Caligula paid his respects in his own way by taking the armor off of Alexander's remains, absconding with the breastplate. That man really had no limits."

They all turned to Callie, who no doubt knew the most about Caligula. As knowledgeable as Nina was about history, she never had the obsession with Roman emperors that Callie had. She had never worn a visage of that emperor's face over her own and called herself Miss Caligula. It was obvious who had the most insight into the crazed Roman emperor.

"That has been a story, yes," Callie said. "But it's never been proven either."

"Proof doesn't always matter," Purdue said. "While it's nice and helpful, often we find things that there was never any evidence for. The things that weren't supposed to exist outside of stories. A story is all we need to at least look at because a story had to have come from somewhere, aye?"

Caligula was no Alexander the Great. Despite being one of the most famous—or, in his case, infamous—emperors to have ever ruled over Ancient Rome. Everyone knew that, but they knew him because of how bad his reputation was. While Alexander the Great declared war on his enemies to conquer them, Caligula declared war on the ocean god Neptune and had his soldiers attack the waves on the shore and collect seashells as trophies of victory; suffice to say, they were two very different calibers of rulers.

"Does it make sense that Caligula would have taken the breastplate?" Purdue asked Callie.

She nodded and slowly started to tell them just some of the strangest things that Caligula did while he was emperor, things that made his grave-robbing of Alexander seem minuscule in comparison.

Apparently, Caligula was obsessed with pleasure and debauchery. His own palace became a brothel that was host to all kinds of things that would make most people uncomfortable. He had enormous boats built that were just used as villas for his biggest parties—referred to as the Nemi ships—that were more lavish than any vessels at the time. Unfortunately, those two ships were destroyed during the Second World War. Outside of his infamous revelry, he had all kinds of strange laws passed that catered to his own insecurities. Because of his balding head, he outlawed anyone standing over him or looking down at him. He also made it so no one could mention goats in his presence since he was afraid that they were talking about him.

The strangest thing he did, though—which made Callie burst into laughter as she recounted it—was that he was trying to make his horse one of the consuls of Rome. In general, he was very close with his steed. The horse's name was Incitatus, and he was given treatment fit for royalty himself. He slept in a stall made of marble and ate from a feeder made of ivory, as well as wore a collar decorated with the most precious of stones that most people would never have been able to afford. Before one of his races, Caligula ordered a mandatory silence throughout the city to prevent his horse from being distracted. The horse was treated almost like an emperor himself, wining and dining with Caligula.

"I don't believe that," Purdue said through his hysterical laughing. "There's no way that it was that bad."

"It was, trust me," Callie said, smirking. "Caligula was cruel to everyone. He would have them tortured and killed on a whim, but his famous cruelty didn't seem to extend to his horse. The one creature that he was kind to."

"Too kind," Nina said. "If only he treated human beings with the same kind of graciousness that he treated his horse with. From what I recall, though, Caligula was far too busy executing people for imagined treason."

"That's true," Callie said. "He wasn't always just eccentric. He was also extremely cruel."

"He sounds like a proper madman that was off his rocker to me," Purdue said. He was always fascinated by ancient people that got up to all kinds of strange things that would be frowned upon in modern society, but Caligula was far too much for him. He was a lunatic. "I hope someone put him down."

"Oh, don't worry about that," Callie said. "Even Ancient Rome got tired of him and his lunacy."

PARANOIA AND PRAETORIANS

Caligula lived in his own world, a place where even the craziest of ideas had merit and could be written into law on a whim. He was known as an unpredictable emperor, a volatile emperor, and, worst of all, a dangerous emperor. Over his reign, everyone from the peasants on the streets to the politicians and imperial guard knew that he was a threat to everyone's safety. A madman should not be the one dictating what happened to Rome. Everyone could agree on that, and those murmurings grew louder with every passing day.

Even Gaius heard them while he still worked closely with the increasingly unpopular emperor. He would have had to cut his own ears off to avoid hearing all of those rumblings. He didn't know what to do about it, if it was possible to even do anything about it. The emperor had dug his own grave with his insane actions that made everyone uneasy. The leader of an empire should not be someone that no one trusted, that seemed not to be sharing the reality that the rest of the world did.

Caligula was no fool, though. He could sense that his people might be starting to grow discontent and might even turn on him. It was in times like that that he seemed particularly glad that they dug up the breastplate of Alexander the Great. If the stories were true, that piece of armor would be able to keep him safe from any physical harm. That was exactly what he needed as his empire turned on him.

Caligula looked out at Rome, the breastplate safely strapped around his torso. He didn't turn to face Gaius when he spoke to him. "I think they may be starting to hate me down there...all those little people...they cannot stand me, can they?"

Gaius didn't want to be the one to give him the unfortunate truth. For all he knew, just being honest would cause the emperor to remove his tongue. He had done worse to people for less. Instead, he opted to try to tell Caligula things that hopefully would not upset him. "You are as popular as ever. The people love you."

Caligula cackled and shook his head feverishly. "Come now, we both know that is not the truth." He held his hand to his ear. "You can almost hear them right now. Do you hear it? All of those whispers of treachery? Listen to how loud they are."

Gaius couldn't hear anything. Of course, he couldn't because that noise was only echoing inside the emperor's mind.

"Come closer," Caligula ordered, waving him toward the balcony. "Come closer, and you will be able to hear them too. It's impossible not to hear them with how loud they're being. They're barely trying to hide it! Come here and listen! Come listen!"

Gaius did as he was bid, just like he always did, and slowly walked over to the balcony's edge where the emperor sat. Even standing out over the city, he still couldn't hear anything but the breeze.

Caligula apparently expected something more. "Ah, see!? You hear it now, don't you!? Listen to their plot! Listen to their scheme! After all I have done for them! After all I have sacrificed for this empire, they still turn on me!"

Gaius couldn't remember anything helpful that Caligula had done for Rome. He especially couldn't remember any sacrifices he had to make. The emperor never gave anything to anyone; he only *took*. All of his endless debauchery and revelry were hardly sacrifices of any kind. He only knew the euphoric joy that he used his power to give himself. He really seemed to think that he was some great, selfless leader when that could not have been further from the truth.

"There is treachery and dishonesty all around me. They know that I am their emperor, but they still conspire to remove me from my rightful place." Caligula's voice was wistful and sad for a moment as he looked out over his people. Suddenly, that sadness turned to rage as he looked at his servant. "Is that what you are doing here!? You are here to kill me and unseat me."

The accusation caught Gaius completely off guard, and he didn't have a chance to defend himself as the emperor grabbed hold of the back of his head and pinned his face down on the balcony's railing, forcing him to look down at the city below. Caligula seemed ready to throw him over the balcony to his death.

"That's it, isn't it? You are here to kill me!"

"No!" Gaius hollered. "That is untrue! I have only ever served you loyally! Everything I have ever done has been to help you and your rule! I swear it on all of the gods!"

Gaius did not want to be killed by the emperor that he had been so loyal to for so long. Then again, perhaps that was his fate. He willingly served a deranged emperor that could not be trusted; doing something like that could always have led to his death.

Thankfully, Caligula seemed to hear him and let go of his grip. He did not apologize and barely seemed to notice who it was that he was about to throw off of a balcony to his death. He was lost in his own thoughts, his own paranoid musings.

The emperor tapped the breastplate he wore with his knuckles and grinned. "It does not really matter. There is nothing that anyone can do to me now that I am wearing this. No one will be able to touch me. This armor will protect me just as if did the great Alexander of Macedon."

Caligula seemed to forget that the breastplate had not been able to save Alexander in the end. It had great power but was not insurmountable. There were ways that death could still find him even when he wore it.

"I should execute them *all*. Every last Roman. Anyone that could even think about killing their emperor. Traitors. All of them."

It wasn't the first time that Gaius had heard Caligula say such horrifying things. His paranoia and lack of self-control made him say all kinds of ideas that shocked and disgusted his servant. The worst part was that Caligula had no limits. He was capable of doing anything—and that included killing every last person under his rule.

Gaius left him to his thoughts on the balcony and listened as the emperor continued to scream at the people sleeping below and then quietly have conversations with the moon high above. The madman was not fit to lead; perhaps he never had been. It was at that moment that Gaius knew that all of those whispers were right. Caligula's reign had to end at any cost.

∼

Gaius had long since decided that it was time to get rid of his master. The emperor was a threat to all of Rome. His position had been compromised, and he needed to be eliminated to save the empire.

The rest of Rome felt the same way, and all of those whispers of discontent had festered into the plots of assassination that Caligula had worried so much about. People wanted the emperor dead, and they were determined to turn him into a corpse.

Gaius, being one of Caligula's personal servants, spent a lot of time with the Praetorian guards. The regiment of guards was sworn to protect the emperor of Rome, but beyond that, they also had to protect Rome itself. It was their duty to defend Caligula, but that was exactly why they needed to be the ones to kill him. Even at his most paranoid, he would never suspect men that had sworn their lives to protect his safety. The Praetorian guards agreed.

"We will need your assistance with this," one of the guards, a man named Cassius Chaerea, said to Gaius on a quiet night when they could speak in private. "You know better than most that slaying this monster is precisely what Rome needs. We need new leadership. We can't rely on Caligula and his madness. The man thinks that he is a god. He kills and torments on a whim. Even his most loyal subjects have had to endure his torture, in one way or another."

Everything that was being spoken out loud was treason. If Gaius wanted to, he could have Chaerea and all of his fellow guards exposed and executed for their duplicitous plot. If they had tried something like that years prior, he would have turned them all in and enjoyed watching them be killed. The problem was that after enduring Caligula's insanity for so long, he agreed with the guards now. He wouldn't turn on them or try to stop them. They were right. Caligula had to die.

"What can I do to be of assistance?"

That night, they put their plan into motion. If all went well, by morning, Rome would never have to worry about Caligula's vileness ever again.

Caligula was in good spirits, just enjoying his Palatine Games beneath the palace. It was a collection of sporting events that seemed to amuse the emperor very much. He was very comfortable enjoying the spectacle, surrounded by his guards and still wearing Alexander's breastplate. In most cases, he couldn't have been safer—but that night, he didn't know just how unsafe he really was.

After the games, they walked back through the dark corridors that led back up to the palace. Caligula led the way, laughing, while Gaius and the Praetorian guards followed closely behind. They exchanged anxious glances in the dark, all ready to make their move. They wouldn't be able to hurt him while he was wearing that breastplate, though, and that was exactly why they had asked Gaius for help to begin with. He was the only person that Caligula seemed to really trust, even if he had threatened to drop him to his death shortly beforehand.

Gaius felt a nudge to his side from one of the guards and knew that it was time.

"Sire...it is late, and all of the guests have departed from the palace. Let us get you comfortable before bed. I can take the breastplate for now and will have it in your chamber for the morning."

Gaius wasn't sure if he was being persuasive enough, but he hoped that mentioning the morning so casually would make him feel safe as if he would make it to morning.

Caligula glanced at his servant, and his expression softened. "Ah, gratitude. I may not always remember your name, but you are always trying to help me. I will reward you for this."

It was hard to hear that, knowing what was coming. The emperor slowly unlatched the straps of the armor with Gaius's help as Gaius pried it off of him. Once it was firmly in his hands and he stepped away from the emperor, he knew that it was time. Caligula had never been more vulnerable.

There, down in the dark beneath the palace, knives were suddenly drawn. The guards that had sworn to protect the emperor were now moving to harm him. They all rushed at him at once, brandishing their blades wildly.

Gaius managed to step out of the way in time to watch the sudden violence unfold.

Caligula let out a shriek that echoed through the stone corridor. He didn't have a chance to even try to defend himself before they were upon him and digging their blades into his body. They were swift and precise in their stabs. The emperor's eyes grew wide but seemed fixed on Gaius and the breastplate in his hands. In that moment, in those fleeting final moments of his insane life, the emperor must have known that Gaius betrayed him. While he was not stabbing him, he was just as guilty of the crime.

The guards stabbed Caligula a total of thirty times. It may have been coincidence or some disturbing intentional recreation of Julius Caesar's death, but Gaius didn't bother to ask. All that mattered was that his crazed ruler was dead and gone.

Gaius took the opportunity to leave with the armor that he had dug up and stolen for Caligula. The emperor would never be able to put him in that compromising position ever again. Rome was safe from that madman. Now all he had to do was figure out what to do with the breastplate of Alexander the Great since Caligula would no longer be needing it.

7

THE NEW FACES

Purdue and the others continued to try to dive deeper into the mind of the deranged emperor, Caligula, but it wasn't exactly easy. It was hard to find any reason or logic in the actions of that ancient madman. They just hoped that they could find something that might point them in the direction of what he might have done with Alexander's breastplate.

Callie suggested that they go to a museum that had some of Caligula's unearthed secrets on display, the Nymphaeum Museum of Piazza.

"It's a newer museum and they have a lot of things belonging to Caligula on display, things that were thought to be lost but were found—like our breastplate hopefully will be. There was a dig for about ten years beneath Horti Lamiani."

"Horti what?" Purdue asked.

"It was one of his pleasure villas, where he spent a lot of his time. He was the emperor for four years but he didn't spend nearly as much time on the throne as he did at places like that, where he could just revel in all kinds of things. After Caligula died, his body was even brought there to be cremated before it was moved. There were legends that his ghost haunted Horti Lamiani."

"Wonderful," Nina said. "So I assume we are going to try to communicate with that ghost then and ask him where he ended up putting the breastplate he stole from Alexander's grave."

"Nothing like that," Callie said. "I just thought that given how recent these things were found from Caligula, it might be the best place to point us in the right direction of where he may have hidden the armor."

Once they arrived, the museum exhibit was impressive. There were a lot of things that had been found at the site that used to be Caligula's favorite villa, but there were no breastplates or any other pieces of armor that could help them in their search.

"I think this is a dead end," Purdue had to admit after some time of looking around.

Callie agreed. "Unfortunately. Sorry. I thought we might find something worthwhile."

"It's not your fault," Purdue said.

He noticed that Callie was looking wistfully over at Nina and Elijah as they were on the other end of the exhibit,

The Guardians of lost time

inspecting things. It was the first time that she and Purdue had been alone since the expedition started—outside of him forcing her to step away from questioning the security guard—and she finally seemed like she didn't have to bite her tongue.

"They still really think that I'm involved with what happened at that museum with those imposters, don't they?"

"I don't think they believe it, and I think they want to believe you. They just don't want to be wrong and be made to look like fools."

"They're looking like fools for doubting me," Callie said. "Because I really had nothing to do with it."

"I believe you," Purdue said. He was sure of that now. After spending more time with her, he couldn't imagine that she had gone back to her old ways. She seemed so genuine in her denial, so upset that she was being painted as a villain again.

It was nice that the exhibit wasn't too crowded. It gave them some peace and quiet, as well as a lack of people staring at them and judging them. Purdue hated having to work around tourists, so it was fortunate that they didn't have to worry about that.

There was the sound of something falling over nearby, and they all turned to find that a row of spears on the wall had spilled onto the ground and a group of newcomers stood over the spears; there were three silhouettes, and they all were wearing masks.

Callie let out an audible gasp and was about to charge at them but Purdue caught her arm and held her back as Nina and Elijah hurried over to regroup with them.

The three masked figures stood before them, all perfectly still, like the statues that their masks were modeled after. Purdue turned to his companions just to make sure that Callie was still standing beside him before looking back to the dark-haired woman standing in the middle of the line of thieves.

"I guess this proves that that's not you, Callie," Purdue said with a smirk.

Callie rolled her eyes. "That's what I have been telling you guys this whole time. I had nothing to do with this."

"Not nothing," the woman in the mask said, stepping forward. "You were a great inspiration to our appearance, Miss Caligula. Without you, Mr. Nero, and Mr. Commodus, we would never have thought to do anything like this. But now, we are just carrying on the work that you started."

"That is a lie," Callie said. "We both know that you are speaking through your ass right now. The Third Triumvirate—the *real* Third Triumvirate—was dedicated to the preservation and restoration of Ancient Rome. The artifacts that we took were going to be used as lightning rods to get others to join our case. We didn't do anything like what all of you pretenders are doing. We didn't destroy the relics that we took."

"You're right," the woman said. "We aren't just copying what the three of you did. We are improving on what you did. Trying to bring back Ancient Rome is asinine. Destroying the things that we no longer need makes much more sense. Then we can move on to better things."

That all sounded very familiar to Purdue—too familiar.

It sounded like the Visionaries.

Purdue voiced that thought just to try to see how this new Third Triumvirate responded. "So, did the Visionaries put you up to this?"

He should have known better than to try to read the expressions of people wearing masks. He couldn't exactly see any change on their faces when he said that name but their silence was honestly answer enough all on its own. They seemed taken aback by his comment, like they were trying to figure out what to say or if they should say anything at all.

He continued, "All of that shit about burning the past to move on to the future sounds like that garbage that those Visionaries were spewing all over the place lately. Those bastards and their obsession with getting rid of artifacts seems to have spread to you too, hmm? Or maybe you are just another group of them that we have to deal with."

After a long moment, the woman spoke up. "The Visionaries are guiding the world into the future...at least the ones that are willing to listen to them into the new days to come. We are simply helping them complete their purpose."

"By becoming a Third Triumvirate?" Purdue laughed. "Please. I can see right through this. Putting on those masks is just a ploy to mess with our heads. A weak attempt at psychological warfare that the Visionaries think will throw us off balance."

"You seem off balance," the lead masked woman said. "So maybe they succeeded."

"We were idiots to try to do what we did as the Third Triumvirate," Callie said. "And you are just making even more of a mockery of the foolish things that we did. I wouldn't care, but both Mr. Nero and Mr. Commodus are dead. You are insulting their memories."

"You should be flattered that we have molded ourselves after you, though we picked far better emperors to put on our faces. I mean, the three of you chose some of the worst emperors in the history of Rome. It is like you were asking to be failures."

That almost made Callie rush up and attack the woman, but Purdue caught her arm and kept her from charging. The woman behind the mask cackled at the sight of that and tapped the visage in front of her true face.

"Me, for instance. Miss Augustus. The first emperor of Rome that set the stage for so many others to follow. And behind me, there is Mr. Aurelius and Mr. Trajan. As you can see, the emperors that we picked to showcase are far better than the disgraceful ones that you chose to represent. Just another example of this Third Triumvirate is an improvement over yours."

"It's all for show!" Callie roared. "The Visionaries just want to make a big spectacle of it and make us look bad! That's all it is! There is nothing really behind it! You don't have the same kinds of dreams that we had! You don't care about Ancient Rome, not really! It's just an excuse to put those masks on your faces."

"So what?" Mr. Trajan boomed behind her. He lumbered forward, towering over everyone else. "Who cares why we wear them? Who cares if we believe in your stupid cause or not? Who cares if we even care about Rome? None of that matters. All that matters is getting noticed and delivering a message that we actually believe in. The world will take notice of the new work that we are doing. They will realize that destroying relics is good for society, just like the Visionaries believe. And then others will follow our example. We are making a statement, setting a trend. The future is coming."

It was all so calculated, so scripted. These three were nothing but mouthpieces for the Visionaries and their beliefs. The new Third Triumvirate were just people that had been brainwashed by the kinds of teachings that Eve Wayneright used to go on stage and preach to people. And they were continuing the work of that stooge, Terrence, that had been burning antique shops to the ground. This was just the next phase in the Visionaries' plans, and they were making it more personal.

"Enough of this," Nina said. "You've been caught. You can drop the act and just come along quietly."

"Caught?" Miss Augustus cackled. "No, we haven't. And we won't be. Especially not by you idiots. But we can't touch you either. The Visionaries have their own plans for the Order of the Black Sun. It's not our job to get rid of you. We have other work that we are supposed to do instead."

Elijah scoffed, "Like what?"

Miss Augustus suddenly pulled out a lighter and clicked it on, releasing a flame in her fingers. She smiled behind that flickering fire. "Like this."

The masked woman tossed the lighter in front of her, setting fire to the rack of sarissa between them. The flames consumed those old wooden spears, creating a wall of fire between the Third Triumvirate and the members of the Order of the Black Sun.

"We are going to find the breastplate of Alexander, and we are going to destroy it before you ever get your hands on it!" she called through the fire. "Alexander is long dead, so there is no reason that that armor has any reason to exist anymore! It will burn just like the rest of history that no longer makes any difference!"

Purdue wanted to rush through those flames and start beating all three of those people to a pulp, but there was no way that they were going to be able to get through that barrier that would burn them alive if they tried. The fire was far too hot as it continued to devour those sarissa.

Elijah fell to his knees in front of the burning spears, watching them disintegrate in the midst of that inferno. There was nothing that hurt the curator more than watching priceless relics be ruined by the hands of people that did not respect them. He was in a great deal of turmoil having to watch that and being absolutely powerless to do anything about it. He would have taken those sarissa spears back to the compound and made sure that they were well preserved. Instead, he had to watch as they were erased from existence.

Through the glow and haze of the flames, they watched the three members of the new Third Triumvirate turn around and hurry down the corridor. They had no intention of being caught. Despite the differences between them and the group that Callie used to be with, they shared their ability to get away with their crimes. But, if they were anything like the last Third Triumvirate, they would make a costly mistake that would trip them up in the end.

∼

"Now do you believe me!?" Callie asked with some irritated exasperation. She had every right to be upset with them and to relish that she was proven to be innocent. It must have felt good to be exonerated after facing so much suspicion. "Well, do you?"

"Of course we do," Purdue said, putting a comforting hand on her shoulder. "Of course."

"Well, there's always the chance that you could be secretly funding their group or something," Elijah said dryly. They couldn't tell if he was joking or not. Purdue was inclined to think that he was still legitimately suspecting Callie.

"I'm not!" Callie said. "Come on, you know I'm not."

"You wanted evidence and proof that she wasn't guilty," Nina said to the curator. "Well, there it was. I'm sorry to have suspected you at all, Callie, but I hope you understand where we were coming from. We just didn't want to end up with a knife in our collective back. I hoped it wasn't you, but we couldn't be too careful."

"You could have just trusted me," Callie said, still obviously feeling a bit angry about the whole ordeal. "That would have been the best way to handle it. Would have saved us all a lot of trouble."

Purdue tried his best to play mediator. "The important thing is that we are all on the same page now. We know what the truth is. This new Third Triumvirate is going to be a problem. No, they are going to be even more than a problem because they are apparently being backed by the Visionaries. I should have realized that they would have some kind of hand in all of this."

"Why, because you antagonized them and threatened to go after all of them?" Nina asked with a little laugh. "Gee, Purdue, it's almost like you make enemies wherever you go that then dedicate their lives to trying to hurt you and everyone you know."

"I am aware," Purdue said. "I tried to counteract that when I left, remember? It's just...well, that didn't work either. But of course I told them I was coming for them. They needed to know that they weren't just going to get away with controlling the world."

"How has that worked out so far?" Elijah asked.

"Admittedly, not great," Purdue said. "And evidently, they are the ones on the offensive right now. This whole Third Triumvirate business was just a way to bait us. To make us doubt our own and to poke at us. They brought back an old enemy to make us feel like failures. For people that want to destroy the past, the Visionaries sure like to dig up old ghosts."

"They can preach about history being useless all they want," Nina said. "But they know that there are things that can be used from the past. They're just hypocrites."

"Hypocrites who are now after the breastplate, too," Elijah said, keeping his focus on the item that he desired so much. "We cannot let that happen. We can't let them keep destroying things that mattered—that still matter."

The work of the Visionaries was like a personal attack on a curator like Elijah. He cared so much about preserving those relics and making sure that no one got their hands on them to ruin them. The Visionaries did not care about the importance of artifacts. They just saw them as junk that should be tossed out and erased. They were everything that Elijah Dane hated about the world, and he was determined to stop them. The breastplate of

Alexander the Great, in particular, being something that he always dreamed of getting his hands on, was something that he especially wanted to protect.

"The Visionaries are not just going after random antique shops and museums anymore. They are doing things that are specifically designed to get in the way of our work. They are trying to cripple the Order of the Black Sun as a whole. This faux Third Triumvirate is just a tool for them to use in this war."

"I hate them," Callie said. "I hate them so much."

"Let's get moving," Elijah said. "There is no time to waste. If they get to the armor before us and destroy it, I will hold each and every one of you field operatives accountable."

Elijah hurried off toward the car, and Nina followed. Callie lingered behind, staring up at the sky in deep thought. It must have been so strange for her to see something of a mirror to who she used to be. She had started the Third Triumvirate but thought that the group of thieves was long buried. Now it had been dug up and waved around in her face to mock her.

Purdue tried his best to be comforting and also wanted to get an understanding of what she was thinking. "It's going to be alright, aye? We will stop them just like we stopped the first Triumvirate, remember?" Of course she remembered, but she didn't say anything. He tried a different approach. "You seemed to be taking a lot of her insults toward the Third Triumvirate to heart..."

"I didn't really enjoy my time in that group," Callie said solemnly. "And, of course, it led me to follow my worst instincts and make some very poor decisions. And it led me into all kinds of trouble and some near-death situations. I did...I did some really awful things when I was wearing that mask. But still, even after all of that...it had been a time when I was really fighting for something. And while I was not exactly friends with Mr. Nero or Mr. Commodus, I still had to watch them die. They didn't deserve what happened to them."

"I get that," Purdue said. "They were still important people in your life, even if you had your reservations about them."

"These people are just going to burn the whole world to the ground, aren't they? They don't care that things mean something, and they don't care about the value and historical significance of any of it. They want it all gone until the only thing left is the things that they can control."

"Aye, that's the Visionaries in a nutshell. And that's the new Third Triumvirate too. They don't care. They never have. And that's why we need to make sure that we stop them. They can keep blaming me for fanning the flames and making things worse when I threatened those bastards, but I don't regret it. People like the Visionaries think they can just run over everything in their path. They needed to know that there was someone standing in their way that wouldn't just let them pass. The Order of the Black Sun that I helped remake stands in existential opposition to those people. We want to protect history. They want to destroy it. That's what it comes down to. We are diametrically opposed."

"Good, because I am the same way with these posers in the masks," Callie said. "If we stop them, we hurt the Visionaries too, right?"

"Most likely," Purdue said. "We will at least remove one of the many appendages that they can use. So it's a win-win if we can stop these bastards and protect the breastplate."

"Then that's what we have to do," Callie said with a nod.

They both wanted to keep their enemies from getting their way. They wanted the Visionaries and the new Third Triumvirate to fail, at least in this one thing. Purdue could feel that she was just as hell-bent on doing some damage to their enemies. That was perfect.

"Are you guys coming or what?" Nina called over. "This is a race, remember?"

That was true—and the race was on.

8

THE NEW TRIUMVIRATE

Miss Augustus was not expecting to come face-to-face with one of the members of the original Third Triumvirate. She knew that the former Miss Caligula was working with the Order of the Black Sun, but she never believed that she would have the distinct opportunity of coming face-to-face. Part of her knew that it was exactly what the Visionaries wanted. That was part of why they had created the new Third Triumvirate to begin with. They were meant to cause strife to their enemies, to plague their thoughts.

"That was annoying," Mr. Trajan growled behind his mask. "They should have given us more warning that those people would be coming to get in our way."

"They wanted them to get in our way, obviously," Miss Augustus said. "The Visionaries sent us there because they knew that they were already there. But don't fret, my friend. They didn't catch us, and they never will. We are protected by our benefactors, and they are protected by nothing. We have more resources than they could ever dream of to get our work done. We will get to Alexander's breastplate before they do. The Visionaries already have people working on possible locations for us to go. There's nothing to worry about. Nothing at all."

"I didn't say I was worried," Mr. Trajan growled again. "I said that I was annoyed. And I am."

Mr. Trajan was a tall, broad, muscular tank of a man, but he was not exactly intelligent. He only had very base-level thoughts and only really took in the information that was in front of him. He couldn't think in hypotheticals or anything like that. He needed concrete things to be right in front of him and refused to think deeply about any of it. He was irritated, and he was going to remain irritated until he beat down their enemies with his bare hands to feel better.

"Miss Augustus is right," Mr. Aurelius said quietly. He was always the shyest of the group and barely ever spoke up. When he did voice his opinion, it was usually just to support an opinion that someone had already presented. He was a follower at heart and always made that obvious. "We will get to the breastplate before they do."

"We should have just killed them right then and there," Mr. Trajan said. "That would have been the best way to handle things. They wouldn't have been able to bother us anymore if they were dead. We wouldn't have to try to beat them to the armor because they wouldn't be able to move. You should have just let me do it."

"It was too much of a risk to get into a fight with them," Miss Augustus said. "Besides, they had the numbers anyway."

"Ha!" Mr. Trajan let out an ugly snort of laughter, shaking his head. "You *really* think that they had the advantage? That they had the numbers? It would take at least three of them to take me on. So I don't think we were as outnumbered as you think."

"I get it, you are big and strong, but that will only get us so far," Miss Augustus said. "The Visionaries chose us because they trusted us to make the best decisions for them. And they told us not to kill them. They aren't ours to—"

"Fine, but we could have at least bruised them up a bit. Broken a few bones. Taught them a lesson."

There was just no way of pleasing Mr. Trajan. It was obvious that the Visionaries had only chosen him because of his physical prowess. It was up to Miss Augustus to be the one to set the tone and make sure that everything was done as instructed. They would be completely lost without her.

Still, she needed to accommodate her colleague a little bit. It was the only way to keep him loyal and listening. "If we just happen to injure them a little during our search for the breastplate, then that will just be collateral damage. Not our fault, I suppose."

Mr. Trajan was obviously smiling behind his mask. "Perfect. That sounds like a plan I can get behind."

Now they just had to wait for the Visionaries to give them another lead and then they would go find and destroy the breastplate of Alexander for them. There was something extra special about finding something like that and then getting rid of it once and for all. When an artifact was lost, there was always a chance that it could be dug up and found later. But once it was gone, there was no getting it back, and all of its significance would burn with it.

"Now, we just wait."

∼

MISS AUGUSTUS'S BACKSTORY

Olivia Marmeno had heard about the Third Triumvirate. Everyone had. Those thieves had made quite the stir when they were going around and stealing from museums. They had become quite the topic of conversation at the time. Everyone wanted to talk about the strange people running around with masks that looked like Roman emperors. The very idea of that had enraptured people's minds and made them fascinated by the group.

She was one of the people that had been so curious about who could be behind those masks and what that must have been like, but she still would never have thought that she would one day be wearing one of those masks—

not until she was approached by a man with a ponytail named Terrence, who had a proposition for her.

Olivia's life had not been very exciting and she had been doing her best not to fall into a pit of despair at the time. She was in a dead-end job where nothing ever happened, and she just kept hoping that the future would be more fruitful for her. She just had to keep telling herself that things would change one day and then make herself believe her own thoughts. Things had to get better. Things would change eventually.

She found solace in a movement that had been slowly gaining traction. She listened to podcasts recorded by a woman named Eve Wayneright, who talked about how the future could be great if people would just let go of the past, and Olivia could not agree more. People needed to stop holding on to things, and she had done her best to purge her house of things that she didn't need. She burned photo albums that she barely ever looked at. She got rid of old clothes and jewelry that she never wore. She didn't need anything that wasn't useful and functional. Sure enough, she found that purging such things gave her a kind of clarity. Her life was improved because she was getting rid of her past.

She became a big follower of Eve Wayneright and her teachings, even becoming a member of her fan club. That must have been why she was approached by Terrence with an opportunity to help Eve and people that shared her beliefs do even more good for the future. She had a chance to be part of something that was going to help other people see things the way that she did. She was going to help show them that burning away the past was the best way to move toward a better future—just like she had done for herself.

Terrence ran his hand through his long hair, smiling at her as he spoke up. "We think that you would be perfect for this opportunity. Eve Wayneright is just the tip of an iceberg that runs so much deeper. We practice what we preach, and we are trying to do that for the whole world. We could use your help and the help of others that truly believe in this great cause."

Olivia had been so willing to listen, so ready to help share the joy of cleansing with the rest of the world.

Terrence just had an important question before they proceeded. "How far are you willing to go to help us spread our message?"

She didn't even hesitate. "As far as I need to go. What you all preach changed my life for the better. I want to help other people feel the same way as I do now."

"And this is your chance to do just that."

Terrence reached into the satchel that he was wearing and pulled out something strange—a mask that depicted someone's face—and offered it to her. She slowly took it into her hands and looked down at the eyeless face looking back at her. It was gray with a mouth frozen into a passive expression.

"What is this supposed to be?"

"It's Augustus Caesar, also known as Octavian, the first emperor of Ancient Rome."

It suddenly clicked for her that she was looking at one of the kinds of masks that those Third Triumvirate people used to wear. She hadn't heard about them or any of their thefts in some time.

"You want me to...to join the Third Triumvirate?"

"Not join them," Terrence said. "No, you will lead them. A new iteration of them. This time, the Triumvirate won't just be stealing relics to protect. You will be taking artifacts so that you can get rid of them. You can help us purge some of the things that the world puts so much stock in, the things that have no purpose sitting behind glass or being out for the public to see. You can clean up the waste of space and make a huge difference, something that can help spread our message even more."

Olivia wanted to help spread that message; that was true. Now she had an opportunity to do something so important to their work. It was more than words and more than speeches and philosophy. She could do some real concrete good in the world.

"Will you help us with this?" Terrence said. "The Visionaries are going to change the world, and you get to be a big part of that change."

"Of course I will," Olivia said, holding the mask tightly in her hands. "I will do whatever I can to make the future of the world better than how it is now."

"Perfect," Terrence said. "We knew that you were a true believer and someone that we could rely on. We will give you two very strong individuals to help carry out our word. Await further instructions. You will throw away the Third Triumvirate from the past and give us one that can help usher in the future that we all want."

It sounded so perfect. Her life was going to change forever and for the better—and she couldn't wait.

When she finally put the mask on, she could feel the power and authority it gave her. It made her see the world even more clearly as if the spirit of Augustus Caesar himself was being channeled through the mask, lending her his power to help her change the world.

While the two accomplices they gave her were maybe not ideal, Terrence continued to tell her that the Visionaries wanted her to lead the way. It was up to her. Mr. Aurelius and Mr. Trajan were both just tools to help her carry out the plan.

With that, and with her new identity as Miss Augustus, Olivia Marmeno was determined to burn away the past and bring about the future that she dreamed about.

9

FINDING A WAY

The hunt for the breastplate of Alexander was back in full swing, but they needed to figure out what Caligula might have done with it after he stole it from Alexander's burial site. With Callie mostly trusted again, everyone convened with her, trying to see if there was anything about Caligula that she knew that might help them figure out what he might have done with the legendary armor.

"I just don't know," Callie said after what felt like hours of musings. "It's not like I knew the guy, and if I did, I still don't think that it would have helped much. He was notoriously irrational and erratic. He literally could have done anything with it."

"But if he went through all of the trouble of digging up the breastplate, wouldn't he have done something of note with it?"

"Not necessarily," Callie said. "He was insane. Maybe he just took it as a joke or got bored with it right away. There's no telling what he actually did with it. And it's not like they kept the best records of things happening back then either, which doesn't help."

That was true. There really wasn't much to go on, especially compared to some of the other things that the Order of the Black Sun went after. It presented a very interesting challenge to have to try to think like some deranged horrible emperor of Rome. To try to get into the head of Caligula wasn't exactly easy. Just from what Purdue had heard about him, he couldn't imagine doing even half of the things that Caligula had done during his lifetime. The sheer level of violence, chaos, and debauchery would have been impressive if it wasn't so utterly horrifying. All they could hope for was that the new Third Triumvirate and the Visionaries were having just as much trouble trying to figure Caligula out too.

They just needed a lead—any kind of lead.

It was time to really dive into research. The four of them all pulled out their phones and laptops and sat around their hotel room, scouring the worldwide web for even the smallest of crumbs that might be able to help point them in the right direction.

Research wasn't Purdue's favorite part of expeditions. He usually preferred the thrill of actually discovering something that was lost. He liked all of the traveling and all of the running around. He enjoyed the scavenger hunt aspect of it. The research was usually the part that bored him, the part that he liked to get over with early, but this expedition had given them no choice but to dive deep into it.

He let out a loud groan so everyone else in the room could hear. Most of them just looked annoyed that he had interrupted all of their reading and scrolling. He tossed his phone aside onto the bed and stretched, letting out a loud yawn.

"I don't know, Elijah, maybe there is no finding the breastplate. And that means that our friends the Visionaries probably won't get to it either. Is there anything else on that wish list of yours that you would be willing to get instead as a consolation?"

Elijah pushed his glasses up the ridge of his nose, blinking hard in disbelief. "That's it? You really give up that easily? All because you are bored and don't like reading? You just can't sit still for a couple of hours?"

"A couple of hours?" Purdue snickered. "It's been almost a day and we are no closer to finding it than we were when we first started looking. My eyes are strained, I've got a headache from staring at the screen, and I'm just starting to think we may be wasting our time on this one. That's not a crime, aye?"

"You might be right," Nina said. "And if we were the only ones looking for the breastplate, I might be inclined to throw in the towel with you, Purdue. But the fact is, we know that there are some very bad people also looking. We can't risk them getting to it. If we gave up and they got their hands on it...you really want that?"

"Thank you, Nina," Elijah said bitterly. "At least someone hasn't decided to just surrender."

"I'm not surrendering," Purdue said. "I'm just trying to be realistic about it. As much as I want to make your dream come true, we have got nothing to work with."

"I might have something," Callie spoke up.

Everyone dropped what they were doing and rushed over to where she was sitting at the hotel room's desk, her computer out in front of her. There was old writing on the screen, a picture of an old scroll that she was examining closely.

"This was an old scroll dating back to the times when Caligula was ruling Rome. It's been translated and studied, detailing a messenger's account of something being moved out of Alexandria."

Alexandria was one of the places where many thought that Alexander had been buried. He had founded the city in Egypt and used it as the capital of his domain in that region, becoming the hub for his naval forces in the Mediterranean. As its name suggested, the city had deep ties to him.

"What else does it say?" Purdue said, finally feeling like they might have a thread to try to follow. "Go on."

"If it's any indication, it talks about a resting place and also about a tunic that was being sent to Caligula."

"A tunic?" Elijah asked, looking disappointed. "A tunic is not armor or a breastplate."

Nina spoke up, offering a comforting alternative. "No, but they might not have wanted to share the details of the delivery in a message, just in case it was intercepted. They might have just called it a tunic to help protect it from prying eyes but also making it clear what it was."

That was a great point that seemed plausible, and they could all feel the energy in the room shift thanks to that idea.

"There is also another scroll that also talks about a tunic," Callie said. "This one dated a few years later. It talks about a tunic being moved from Caligula's palace back to where it was found. They apparently weren't comfortable holding on to it after Caligula's death."

"How did that crazy bastard die?" Purdue asked. He hadn't seen that detailed yet in any of his research.

"His own guards killed him."

"They weren't very good at their job then, aye?"

"Or they cared about safeguarding the people of the empire more than they cared about protecting their deranged psychopathic boss," Nina said.

That was fair. Caligula couldn't have been the easiest person to work for. He probably had his servants and guards doing all kinds of messed up things. It was no wonder that they decided that enough was enough and took him out for good.

"The senate was in on it too. It was a conspiracy to get rid of a terrible ruler and try to restore the Roman Republic," Callie said. "It didn't work out, but it was a valiant effort."

Elijah didn't care about how or why Caligula was killed. He just cared about what he had taken from that burial ground. "So the tunic...that we assume is the breastplate...it was sent back to Alexandria after Caligula's death?"

"According to this, yes," Callie said. "But it's impossible to know for sure."

"Impossible to know unless we go there and find it," Purdue said with a smile.

The optimistic energy growing in the room surged, and they could all feel the electricity that helped them all get to their feet. They finally had a chance to put down all of the research and take action to go try to find it.

In short, they finally had a lead and were hopefully going to follow it straight to the armor.

～

The Visionaries were finally in touch with the new Third Triumvirate. It had taken long enough, but Miss Augustus knew not to complain. She didn't have to do any of the research herself, after all. She just had to wait until she was told where she and her team should go next. The phone ringing to give them the news was a wonderful sound, though; she had been getting so tired of Mr. Trajan's anxious pacing and stomping around impatiently.

The voice on the phone spoke with some good news. "We have an update on the breastplate of Alexander. We have found documents indicating that the armor was brought to Alexandria and may still reside there."

That was a long distance away from where they currently were, and Miss Augustus was not very fond of traveling. She wouldn't complain, though, especially not to her superiors. She needed to keep doing as she was asked and doing it well so that the Visionaries knew they could rely on her. This was her only chance to impress them, and she was going to do everything she could to do that.

"What about the Order of the Black Sun?"

"From what we have seen. They are going to be there as well. You must beat them to the armor and make sure that they do not get it. If they do, we will have very little chance of destroying the breastplate. They will put it away with all of their other trophies, never to be seen again."

No one wanted that. The Order of the Black Sun was so determined to hold on to things that the world didn't need anymore. They hid those items in places that not even the Visionaries could get to. That was so much worse than museums or even government facilities that housed relics and pieces of history. The Visionaries could get to those places, but for some reason, the Order of the Black Sun's collection was untouchable.

"We will get there first," Miss Augustus promised and hung up the phone.

"Where are we going?" Mr. Aurelius asked curiously.

"The city of Alexandria in Egypt," she said. "That is the next possible place where the armor might have been taken."

"And are they going to be there too? The Order of the Black Sun?" Mr. Trajan spat on the floor. "Good. I want a chance to pull them apart."

"We don't touch them, remember?"

"You don't have to," Mr. Trajan said. "But just try to stop me."

"I won't try to stop you," Mr. Aurelius said, as meek and submissive as ever. "But don't forget that we are supposed to bring them back to the Visionaries alive."

"I haven't forgotten, but I don't think they'll mind an exception."

Miss Augustus wasn't so certain about that, but she knew better than to try to convince Mr. Trajan of anything. Once his mind was made up, he wasn't able to see any other possibilities. He was like a bull that couldn't be stopped once it saw red.

10

THE POWER OF THE PAST

The flight from Italy to Egypt on Purdue's private jet was much less intense than the last flight they had. Now that they knew that Callie was not involved with the new Third Triumvirate, so much of the tension had been sucked out of the plane, putting all of them at ease. No one was happier about it than Callie, who was finally being treated like a full-fledged member of the group again.

Everyone was sharing stories about adventures they had gone on, ones that Callie had not had a chance to be a part of. It was a wonderful conversation that felt like a chat between friends, something that was about work but was littered with laughs and nostalgic reminiscing. Callie just seemed happy to be trusted with those stories.

"Well, there was the time that we got caught up on that flying machine of Leonardo da Vinci's..." Purdue said. "It was this huge contraption...a lot different than this airplane that we're in right now. Much more...crude, aye, crude."

"The worst," Nina said. "And that was after *The Mona Lisa* had been stolen."

"And after we were nearly killed by automatons he built. Who would have thought that Leonardo da Vinci's famous inventions were built for longevity and still completely functioning nowadays?"

Elijah yawned in his seat. "They don't build them like they used to."

"And let's not forget about all of the shit that I had to go through when Julian Corvus stole all of my money, kidnapped my friends, and ransacked my trophy room. That bastard took everything from me." There was a time when Purdue would have had trouble talking about that very traumatic period of his life, but enough time had passed where he could actually acknowledge it. It was probably because Julian was finally beaten and trapped deep beneath Chicago, where he couldn't haunt him anymore. "I had to buddy up with pirates to find a bunch of gold just to try to get enough money to try to get my actual money back. It was a mess, aye. A very big mess. And that wasn't even as messy as getting involved with an occult bookshop owner trying to protect a magic book. Once you bring all of that occult business into it... that's when it gets impossibly messy."

"It's nice that you at least managed to get everything back," Callie said. "Or at least...enough of it."

"Oh yes, eventually, but that was after a half dozen near-death experiences and traversing a transporting Mayan Temple."

Callie looked like she wasn't sure if he was joking about that or not. If only she had been there to see it.

"You are boring her to tears telling her about things that she wasn't even involved in," Nina said. "You think she wants to hear about you patting yourself on the back and praising yourself for all of your many victories? No one wants to hear that. Not even you, Purdue."

That got everyone laughing.

Nina continued, "No, if we are going to talk about something that happened a while ago, we need to talk about Caesar's sword."

Callie's face grew bright red and she tried to hide her face in her hands. Nina stood up and lightly tapped her with her foot. "Oh, come on, why don't you want to talk about that? You weren't there for that one, Purdue. My first time leading a field mission."

"Oh, I remember, aye," he said. "And the first time that we ever encountered the Third Triumvirate."

"Remember that?" Nina laughed, prodding at Callie with her foot until Callie dared to look from her hands. She looked absolutely humiliated and embarrassed. "You remember, right? You and me fighting in the Coliseum, swinging around weapons and fighting to the death. We were practically gladiators at the time."

"I remember," Callie said with an awkward smile. "Unfortunately."

"Were you really going to kill me during all of that? Just because I wasn't going to let you and your friends somehow bring Ancient Rome back?"

"It was a different time," Callie said with a little laugh. "I swear, I was a completely different person. I was so wrapped up in all of the things that the three of us talked about that I was willing to do anything…and yes, that includes maybe killing you too. I really can't apologize enough for that."

"It's water under the bridge now," Purdue said and turned to Nina. "Right?"

"Of course," Nina snickered. "Really, you were right that you have done so much to prove yourself. We are the ones that should keep apologizing to you. You have been—"

"Before we get all sentimental," Elijah cut in, sitting up in his seat. "Can we just acknowledge all of the artifacts that you all have gone after, and then for one reason or another, you don't bring them to me in the deep vault?"

No one wanted to talk about that, but the curator was very adamant and very excited to finally vent his frustrations. "I could name at least twenty off the top of my head. The da Vinci flying machine, for one thing."

"That wouldn't have fit," Purdue reminded him. "You could have never gotten that into the deep vault. Besides, it crashed."

"You always have an excuse to show up without anything for me," Elijah said, pointing his finger at them. "Remember that story you weaved about why you had to take that pearl out of the vault and bring it back to the ocean to give to Poseidon?"

"I did have to do that!" Purdue cackled but did take some offense. "It's absolutely the truth! You saw what that pearl could do for yourself? It practically destroyed the plumbing in the compound! Poseidon wanted it back!"

Elijah wasn't convinced. "I can believe a lot of things, but a god of the sea forcing you to bring that pearl back to the ocean isn't one of them. That pearl should have stayed in the deep vault where it belonged."

"Then the whole compound would be flooded."

Elijah didn't care. "At least it would have been safe."

Their conversations about all of those expeditions and the prizes that they found from them continued all the way to Egypt. Those talks were full of fond memories, difficult times, and a lot of laughs to help them get through all of it. It was amazing how much joy reminiscing could bring.

"You know what's funny?" Nina asked. "If the Visionaries got their way, we wouldn't even be talking about any of this. They want to destroy all of those things that we spent so long finding. Can you imagine?"

"They just hate fun," Purdue said.

Callie nodded along. "They definitely do. I don't think that is up for debate."

The closer they got to Alexandria, the more excited Nina became. She took one of the window seats and stared out at the clouds and what waited beneath. She stayed there the rest of the time until the plane started to descend toward their destination.

Purdue hoped that Alexandria would be where that breastplate had ended up, but they wouldn't know until they actually got to start the search. Maybe someday, the story of their search for the breastplate of Alexander would be one of the stories that they talked and laughed about—only time would tell.

11

THE CITY OF LOST SITES

Alexandria was as beautiful as Purdue hoped that it would be. He stared out at the Mediterranean and just took in the sight of its shimmering waters. He had been all over the world, but there was always something special about a city that had been around for so long, that had been the site of so many significant events and gone through millennia of history.

Nina made sure to remind them all of that history as they made their way to where they would be staying. Nina, like always, spoke about history with so much passion and contagious excitement as she looked around.

"Alexandria, as the name suggests, was founded by its namesake, Alexander of Macedon. It was 332 B.C. when Alexander established the city during the early stages of his campaign against the Persian Empire. This city was meant to be the capital of the dominion that he had over

Egypt and would function as an important naval base given its location..."

That wasn't surprising, considering that the Mediterranean Sea was right there. It didn't take a genius to see the advantages of having a base there. Maybe Alexander wasn't as smart as he probably used to think he was; Purdue liked to think that he might have given that ancient king a run for his money. Sure, he had been so *great* at the time, but who knows how Alexander would have fared in the modern world? He might not have stood a chance.

"Alexandria has always been an important trading port and remains so to this day..."

While Purdue appreciated the history refresher, he knew that it was just how Nina coped when she was nervous on an expedition. She liked to talk about the things that she knew so much about to keep from focusing on the elusive thing that she was trying to find. It could be a little irritating, but he understood why she felt the need to do it.

"Unfortunately, there are parts of the city that did not survive the test of time like their trading ports did. The Library of Alexandria, for one thing..."

Purdue didn't need to be told what that was. Everyone who knew anything about ancient history had heard about the destruction of the Great Library that happened two thousand years ago.

Nina continued. "All of that collected knowledge was lost that day, none of it having ever been able to be recovered. It's really tragic when you think about it."

"Sounds like something the Visionaries would have loved," Purdue said. "They would have lit the matches themselves to see all of that written history go up in flames, eh?"

Nina brushed aside those kinds of theories about their present day, still focused on the history. "Some sources said that somewhere around forty thousand scrolls burned when the Great Library was destroyed."

Elijah looked disgusted by the discussion. "Such a waste. The Alexandrians should have done a better job keeping all of it safe."

Purdue had to laugh. "Yes, yes. We all know how much better of a job you would have done, Elijah, but give them a break, eh? It's not like they had the technology and safeguards back then that the deep vault has now."

Elijah rolled his eyes. "It still probably could have been prevented. Most things can."

"How did the fire even start?" Callie asked from the back of the group.

Nina shrugged. "No one really knows for sure. Like so much of history, there isn't a definitive answer."

"Maybe the page that said who did it burned too," Purdue said cheekily, but no one laughed.

Nina ignored him like she always did. "Some say the Christians burned it when they made their way to the city since some of its contents might have been considered pagan...well, a lot of the contents, really."

Elijah snorted. "That makes sense."

Purdue continued with his theory, half-joking but also entertaining the idea. "Or, as I said, what if the Visionaries really were around back then, already trying to destroy the past to move on to the future or whatever?"

Again, no one seemed overly enthused by the possibility —and they didn't find it funny either.

Nina at least addressed it. "I doubt it. The Visionaries we are facing now reek of more modern sensibilities. The disrespect of truth and history, for one thing. The ignorance and reliance on technological advancements and idealized futures. People back then at least revered things more than the Visionaries do. No...the people we are up against haven't been around long. I would put money on that."

"How much money?" Purdue said with a wink. The fact was, she could jeer at his theory all she wanted but so far there wasn't anything that flat-out disproved the possibility of the Visionaries existing back then. He wasn't fully behind the thought either, but it was fun to prod at his historian friend a little.

Nina pointed toward the coast. "The Great Library wasn't the only thing that was lost. One of the Seven

Wonders of the World was here, too, at one point. The Lighthouse of Alexandria."

"And what was so special about that?" Purdue asked.

"At the time, it was one of the tallest man-made structures in the world. And obviously it was meant to help guide sailors to shore. It stood for quite a long time before a number of earthquakes tore it down to ruins."

"All I'm hearing is that this city has horrible luck with its significant monuments, aye? Think of all of that lost tourist revenue nowadays if the library and the lighthouse were still standing. Alexander should have set the place up for better longevity when he founded it."

"Hopefully his breastplate isn't among the things that were lost here..." Elijah said gravely, the excitement being sucked out of his body before their eyes.

It was easy to forget that the whole reason that they were even there was to try to help the curator fulfill his desire to be able to get his hands on the armor. He was the one that wanted it more than any of the others. No matter what its historical significance was, no matter what power it might possess, Elijah wanted it just so he could inspect it for himself, with his own hands and with his own eyes. That was what was important, and they couldn't lose sight of that.

"I'm sure it will be here," Purdue said, trying to offer some bit of comfort.

Nina pointed ahead at an old fortress on the coastline, looming over the glimmering waters. "That's our destination. Fort Qaitbay...where the Lighthouse of Alexandria used to stand."

"You think that's where the breastplate might be?" Elijah asked, glancing at the structure with growing curiosity.

"The breastplate was said to have been brought back beneath the light, remember? It would make sense for that to be talking about the lighthouse...which no longer stands, but that fort was built in the spot where it used to be. If it was beneath the lighthouse—"

"Then it's beneath the fort now," Purdue finished. "Makes sense to me. It's not much to go off of, but we have gone off less before and found success."

"Exactly," Nina said. "It is worth seeing for ourselves."

They continued their approach toward the fort, ready for whatever lay ahead of them—and hopefully they were closing in on the famous piece of armor.

～

The new Third Triumvirate wasn't in Alexandria to sightsee. None of them cared about the Great Library that burned to the ground. No one cared about the lost lighthouse that once helped ships find harbor. The only thing that they cared about was the breastplate that they were tasked with finding and destroying. That was their goal, and they did not intend to fail. The Visionaries would be so pleased by their success.

They were on their way to one of the possible destinations when they received a text message from the Visionaries. Miss Augustus opened her phone and nearly let out a yell when she saw what was written on the screen. **Remember. The Order of the Black Sun is ours to kill. Avoid them if possible. If confronted, do not use lethal force.**

Miss Augustus casually showed her phone to the lumbering Mr. Trajan beside her. He snorted and shook his head, grinding his teeth. "That's so stupid. If there is an obstacle, then we should get it out of our path."

"Or just leap over it," Mr. Aurelius offered calmly. "Just saying. Violence is not the only option, Trajan."

"From my experience, violence is usually the only thing that gets you actual results in the long run. Wasting so much energy avoiding a fight will just make you weak when one finally comes."

"I didn't expect such poetry to come out of your mouth," Mr. Aurelius said. "But the point remains. We have been given instructions and we should follow those instructions to the letter, whether we like them or not. You have trusted the Visionaries this far. No need to doubt them now."

"I don't doubt them," Mr. Trajan said defensively. "I see where they are coming from. Of course they want to be the ones to finish those bastards off. But that can't be the smartest thing to do."

It was funny hearing Trajan making judgments about other people's intelligence, considering that he had proven to be a rather shortsighted individual whose brawn far outweighed his brain.

"Fort Qaitbey is not far from here," Mr. Aurelius said. "That seems to be the most likely place that Caligula had the breastplate brought back to, according to our sources. So we go there, and we get it. The Visionaries reward us and they will probably bring us even deeper into the fold, architects of the future."

That sounded good to Miss Augustus, but she wasn't going to get her hopes up too high. She didn't want to be let down, not after all of the traveling they had done up to that point. Whether they were going to kill them or not—and she was adamant that they wouldn't—the Order of the Black Sun could be close by. They would have to decide what they were going to do about that when the time came. Hopefully, if all went well, they would never see them during the rest of the search, so they wouldn't have to argue over what to do. All she could really hope for was to have a peaceful rest of their journey without any more fighting. They would get the breastplate, destroy it, then leave the Order of the Black Sun to the Visionaries.

Unfortunately, she knew life was never that easy.

12

WHERE THE LIGHTHOUSE ONCE STOOD

Fort Qaitbey was impressive in its own right, even if it didn't actually house the breastplate of Alexander.

Nina continued to be their tour guide on their visit to Alexandria, running her hands along the wall of the fort and explaining some of its history. "After the lighthouse toppled in 1303, it was some time until anything was done with this place. It was left in ruins...but those same ruins were used as part of the construction of this fort to help protect the port from enemies coming from the sea."

"Or perhaps to protect a powerful artifact inside, aye?" Purdue asked, hopefully.

"Maybe," Nina said. "We should explore some of the chambers within and see if we can get below."

That sounded like a plan. They knew that the armor Alexander the Great wore wasn't going to just be laid out in the open for anyone to find. It would be hidden somewhere where the tourists and visitors to the fort would never have found it.

"I'll lead the way," Elijah said, taking charge. It was so unlike him to be the leader of a group or to be the first one through a door. He was typically so much more reserved and disinterested than that, but given what they might be close to finding, he was determined to be the one that got their first.

No one argued with that, though, and Elijah took them inside the fort, where they looked for any hidden chambers or entryways that might be hard to see.

It was not the first time that Purdue and Nina especially had gone into a fortress to try to find something hidden. He was reminded of a journey to the island of Rhodes long ago, during their search for the Spear of Destiny. Hopefully this fortress wouldn't bring them as much danger as that one did, considering Rhodes was the place where they first met Julian Corvus. So much had happened since then, so many victories and losses, and everything in between. And yet, despite all of that, Purdue and Nina were still standing and were in a much better position than they were back then. Hopefully, this fort would be just as fruitful with information as that one had been.

Purdue decided to ask one of the tour guides about the breastplate of Alexander, just in case they could provide any possible hints of its location or if it was even in the fort at all. He spoke with a nice young woman about it, hoping for something that they could use.

"Excuse me," Purdue said with a smile. "I had someone tell me once that Fort Qaitbey is home to some artifacts that used to belong to Alexander the Great. Is there any truth to that or is it all a bunch of shit that someone was spewing?"

The tour guide didn't have the best answer, at least not the one that he was really hoping for. "Unfortunately, Fort Qaitbey does not have anything like that, I'm sorry to say. If you are looking for information pertaining to the founder of the city, Alexander, then one of the number of museums we have here might be your better option. I am sure that they have much more information about him."

"Thanks," Purdue said without any actual appreciation. He hoped that she wasn't right. Then again, if a piece of armor was secretly hidden within the confines of the fort, he doubted that the people working there would be aware of it.

They searched for hours, thoroughly inspecting every wall in every chamber. The workers that walked by gave them some peculiar looks at first, but Purdue was able to smooth over any confusion and convince them that they were not up to anything that would cause any damage to the fort. He knew that sometimes people doubted some of his talents, but he had always been impressed by his own powers of persuasion.

Finally, after hours and hours of hopeless searching, Elijah let out a gasp and pushed in a stone in one of the walls. A small part of the wall pushed forward and revealed an opening. They all gathered around him and stared at a dark corridor that had been revealed. The fort apparently held more secrets than they thought, and ones that the people that worked there probably weren't aware of either.

Purdue had to admit that he had his doubts about Fort Qaitbey. "Well, that's something... Who wants to go first?"

"After you," Nina said, pushing him forward into the newly discovered corridor. He didn't particularly like to go first when he was entering a new location. There was always a chance that there would be traps and he never wanted to be the one to set them off. Still, he didn't have much of a choice, being shoved down the dark corridor. It was a narrow space, and they all muttered as they slid their way through.

When Purdue reached the end that opened up into a chamber, he saw something he didn't expect to see and let out a series of swears that alerted his friends behind him. Nina couldn't see past him and kept trying to shove him out of the way.

"What's wrong? What is it?"

"See for yourself," Purdue said, making way for his allies to also see what he saw.

They were just as surprised to see the three masked thieves standing in the chamber.

~

THE LAST TASK

Despite coming into possession of the blessed breastplate of Alexander the Great, Caligula still could not evade his enemies. He was not wearing that armor when they came for him and when he was slain.

Gaius would not miss him. He had been a loyal servant to a madman and was hoping that the next emperor he served would not be as insane as Caligula. Still, he had been given one last task by his late master. If anything ever happened to him, he needed to bring Alexander's armor to the same place where all of Caligula's treasures were kept, a place so few people knew about.

It was not the first time that Gaius had gone to that hidden chamber in the middle of the night. Anytime that Caligula had something that he wanted to hold on to, he would order Gaius to bring it to the vault where he could view it at leisure. Though, Gaius could never recall a time when he brought something of actual value there. The treasures that Caligula held on to were the remnants of some of his most unhinged conquests and darkest celebrations, hardly anything of real value.

Gaius considered taking the armor elsewhere. He didn't owe the emperor anything, so he could have sold it or brought it somewhere where it would actually be appreciated. It was not about loyalty to his late master; it was more that he had no idea where else to actually bring it. There was nowhere else for it to go, at least nowhere that seemed safe. He would put it with the rest of Caligula's secret trove, at least for the time being, until he could figure out a more fruitful alternative.

Gaius never had the chance to move the breastplate once he brought it to Caligula's hidden vault. He grew ill not long after and never had the strength to go and bring the armor somewhere else. Caligula had stolen that breastplate and, even in death, continued to hold on to it along with many of the other things that he prized in his life.

Gaius was the only one that knew its location. Prior to his death, he wrote it down on a scroll and had a friend bring it to Alexandria to hopefully get them to find the breastplate and bring it back to where it belonged—with Alexander the Great in his resting place.

13

DEFYING ORDERS

There they were again, all three of them still wearing those stone-faced masks. They all turned to see them come in and it was impossible to know if they were surprised or not. They must have been.

Purdue took the lead. "It must be a very small world for all of us to keep running into each other. Either that or all three of you bastards think that you actually have a chance of getting to the breastplate before we do."

"We got here first, didn't we?" Miss Augustus said coldly.

Purdue couldn't help but laugh. "I suppose you did. How did you manage that? Your Visionary friends must have a lot of money and influence. It wasn't easy figuring out that we had to come here."

"Or maybe the Visionaries just know how to use their wealth more effectively than you do. Don't pretend like you're not incredibly rich yourself, David Purdue. But just because you have money and influence doesn't mean that you know how to use it. You clearly do not. As you can see, we have laid claim to this area to search so you all can just leave."

"There's no 'laying claim' to anything. That's not how this works. This is obviously your first time on one of these searches."

The biggest member of the new Third Triumvirate, Mr. Trajan, stepped forward, practically shoving Miss Augustus out of the way. They could hear his heavy breathing behind the mask as he cracked his knuckles menacingly. He certainly looked big enough to probably dominate a physical fight, but Purdue had been through enough scraps to know that he might still be able to take him on. Size was not everything.

"I kept saying that all of you would just be irritating and that we should take you out while we had the chance. That still stands, and I think now would be the perfect time."

Miss Augustus was not on board with his plan. "That is not what we were instructed—"

"We were instructed to destroy Alexander's breastplate!" Mr. Trajan roared, his deep voice booming. "And we cannot do that with these people constantly getting in our way. I'm sure our superiors would understand. They might even thank me when I deliver David Purdue's head to them."

He made that threat so casually. He obviously meant it. That giant of a man fully intended to tear Purdue's head clean off of his shoulders and deliver it as a gift to the Visionaries. He looked like he could, given his hulking size. He stomped forward, ready for a fight that none of the Order of the Black Sun was prepared for.

Purdue knew for a fact that Elijah Dane was not the best in a fight. He knew that Nina could handle herself but would prefer not to have to get into a scuffle. That meant that it was really down to himself and Callie to handle the combat. She had been a thief that had to fight her way out of plenty of situations, and Purdue had been in enough fights to just inherently become pretty good at defending himself. Still, neither of them would probably be able to stand up to that man on their own.

"Stop," Miss Augustus ordered.

Mr. Trajan's approach came to a halt, but he looked more than ready to take the next step and more than a little annoyed that he had even been interrupted. He craned his head to look back at his accomplice. "What is it?"

"New information," the masked woman said, holding up her phone. "The Visionaries have been digging up more information, and from what they're saying, a rumor was spread that he returned the breastplate, but that was only a cover story. He really had someone bring it to some secret vault of his. That servant did leave the actual location of the vault with someone in Alexandria...and the Visionaries just found an image of that scroll and what was written..."

"That sounds more like him," Callie said under her breath, being the only Caligula expert in the room. "He would do anything he could to make sure that people did not have an easy time. He enjoyed it when other people suffered."

Miss Augustus kept looking at her phone as she walked up to Mr. Trajan and whispered something in his ear, far too quiet for any of Purdue or his allies to overhear. He was curious about whatever information she had just given. They needed to get their hands on her phone somehow.

"Brilliant," Purdue said. "So we can all just get our things and leave without any kind of a scrap, aye? Why fight over something that isn't even here?"

Mr. Trajan was undeterred even with the news. "Because if we don't put an end to you now, you are just going to show up at wherever that secret vault of Caligula's is, and then we will be in this predicament all over again. I would prefer to end it right here and now. Then we can look for that vault at our own leisure."

"Or we could work together," Purdue said, knowing that would never happen.

Mr. Trajan moved to come for them again, but the masked woman grabbed hold of his bulky arm. Miss Augustus was still trying to get him to refrain from trying to hurt them, but the huge man was not having any of that.

"I told you...I'm putting a stop to this race right now."

With a casual flick of his arm, he got out of her grasp and nearly flung her to the floor when he did. Miss Augustus was not pleased about that, shaking her head as she got to her feet. "Fine. You have it your way, then. But Mr. Aurelius and I will have no part in that kind of insubordination. The Visionaries will know who obeyed them and who didn't."

"Works for me," Mr. Trajan growled. "They'll also know who really helped get rid of their enemies for them...and it wasn't you two."

Miss Augustus and Mr. Aurelius hurried out of the chamber without another word, leaving Mr. Trajan alone with the four members of the Order of the Black Sun. Despite their superior numbers, none of them seemed overly confident that they could beat him. They had more people, but their shared mass was barely greater than his. Worst of all, considering they knew nothing about the masked giant's past, they couldn't gauge how experienced a fighter he was. For all they knew, he had spent his life fighting and could beat them all with ease. Maybe that was the case since he was so confident that he could put an end to them then and there.

It was impossible to read his expression behind his mask, but Purdue got the distinct impression that Mr. Trajan was happy. He seemed like the type of man that just enjoyed fighting and proving his own strength to himself and to others.

"So which of you will be first, hmm? We read up on each of you. The Visionaries know all about you people. Is it going to be the rich boy with the big mouth, David Purdue? Or how about the woman that wastes her time on all of that historical bullshit, Dr. Nina Gould? Come on, Doc, you must really hate us for everything we are doing to your precious history. Or how about you, Miss Caligula, or whatever your actual name is? Aren't you mad at us for perfecting what you and your friends started?"

"That's one way of putting it," Callie said. "But I definitely don't think that you perfected anything."

"And then there's you...the scrawny guy with the glasses. You're their curator, right? If you were smart, you would turn over all of those items that you have to the Visionaries. Watch them destroy them all so you never have to worry about them again. That would be liberating, right?"

Elijah remained unfazed, but Purdue could see the anger behind those glasses. He really hated what the Visionaries were doing, defiling artifacts, but he especially hated that they were getting in the way of one of the items that he wanted the most.

"I'm so sick of you people," Elijah muttered.

"What was that?" Mr. Trajan snorted, leaning in. "Did you say something, tiny?"

"I just said that I am sick of you people."

Without another word, Elijah threw a punch that knocked Mr. Trajan in the side of the head, nearly smacking the mask right off of his face. He staggered a few steps back, a little surprised by the sudden strike. When he regained his footing, though, he started to laugh.

"There it is! That's what I wanted. I guess you are the one brave enough to go first. I hope you don't mind dying first, then."

Purdue was surprised to see Elijah striking first, but then again, the curator could get very angry when it came to protecting relics. He didn't take kindly to people that had ill intentions for things that were irreplaceable. All the Visionaries and their cronies did was ruin the things that Elijah loved. It was no wonder he was willing to draw first blood.

"There's four of us and one of you, mate," Purdue said. "I don't think that you should be so eager to fight."

"There are about to be less than four of you," Mr. Trajan snickered.

They all knew better than to try to fight him one at a time. His superior strength would break through each of them one by one. The best chance they had was to combine their efforts, so all four of them rushed him at once, trying to swarm him before he could hurt any one of them. It was hard to tell with the mask on, but given how he stopped and planted his feet, Mr. Trajan seemed a little alarmed by how they all piled onto him.

Still, even together, his strength was overwhelming. They couldn't hold him down for very long. The more they jumped on him, the angrier he got, and the angrier he got, the stronger he seemed to be. His growls of frustration turned into a primal war as he threw his arms out and knocked all of them in different directions, throwing them off of him and freeing himself from their grasp.

"None of you want a fair fight, then?" Mr. Trajan snarled. "You are too scared to fight me one-on-one, so you decided to ambush me instead? Not that that helped much. It's still not fair. You would need at least ten more people to even start to get on my level."

"You really are so full of yourself," Purdue said, climbing to his feet. "What is it with you big, tall brutes that convince yourselves that you are indestructible? I've beaten people like you before. I've seen giants like you fall over like trees. What's the old saying? The bigger they are, the harder they fall?"

"I might fall," Mr. Trajan said as he stepped toward him, "but I will always get back up. The Visionaries really didn't want us to kill you, Purdue. They wanted you for themselves. They probably would have tortured you. They probably would have cut you into little pieces. You should be relieved that it's me and not them. I'm just going to get the job done and then give them your head."

"Why my head?" Purdue said, staggering a little bit. That hit he gave them did more to him than he thought. "Why not something more interesting? My foot? How about that? You can give it to them after you remove it from your ass."

Despite trying to muster some resistance, Purdue knew that he would get beaten down easily by that overwhelmingly large man. It was like being a child trying to fight a full-grown gorilla. He wouldn't stand a chance against him. He looked at the others that were starting to get up and realized that they needed a better plan than trying to fight Mr. Trajan head-on. The good news was that they were closer to the exit than he was.

"Come on! Up! All of you! Let's go!" Purdue started to run toward the corridor and the way out. Nina, Callie, and Elijah looked confused at first but quickly followed when he passed them.

"Hey!" Mr. Trajan roared. "Come back and fight me, you cowards!"

They could hear him stomping after them as they rushed down that narrow, dark corridor that had led them into the hidden chamber. They didn't dare look back at the behemoth that was on their heels. They pushed their way through the opening that they found in the wall back out to the main part of the fort. Before they kept going, though, Elijah decided to try to push that hidden part of the wall back into place and close it on their pursuer. That hidden opening started to close as Mr. Trajan started to come through it. He held the rock wall at bay as it tried to close on him. Their plan to trap him inside hadn't gone quite according to plan.

The huge man used all of his strength to keep the wall at bay. He glared at them as he kept himself from being trapped. "Look at all of you. Running for your lives. Just wait until I catch you. Just you wait."

None of them had any intention of waiting.

"There still might be time to catch the other two," Nina said. "Let's go!"

The four of them hurried away from Mr. Trajan as he started to push his way out of the closing space. They weren't going to stand there and wait for him to get out—and it definitely seemed like he would. They ran out into the courtyard and looked around at the small crowd of tourists, but none of the people they saw looked like Miss Augustus or Mr. Aurelius. And if they had taken off their masks, then they wouldn't be able to recognize them anyway.

"Damn it!" Elijah kicked the dirt. "We were so close. Whatever she found out…it'll probably get them to the breastplate before we can make it there. It's over."

"Not necessarily," Nina said. "She said something to Mr. Trajan. Maybe she told him where they needed to go. If we can get him to tell us—"

"How are we supposed to do that?" Elijah asked. "I don't think he is just going to share that information with us out of the goodness of his heart."

"I didn't say anything about the goodness of his heart, but maybe we could force him to tell us...or convince him to, I don't know."

"First, we would have to stop him from killing us, aye," Purdue said, turning around and finding that the large masked man was coming out of the fort and was just about to spot them. "If that's the plan, then we need to do it now because he is about to come over and kill us."

"In front of these people?" Elijah asked.

"I don't think he cares who sees," Callie said. "He doesn't seem like the type to care about whether or not he gets into any trouble."

Purdue had an idea and started to guide everyone toward the towers of the fort. "Go on this way! We gotta get up to the roof."

Everyone did as he instructed and ran back inside the fort, hurrying up the staircases and making their way to the rooftop. They didn't dare stop or slow down, knowing that he wasn't far behind. They finally got up to the roof of the fort and waited for Mr. Trajan to catch up. When he did, he was breathing heavily but was moving in a dangerous, predatory manner.

"Look at this. There is nowhere to run now."

"We're done running," Purdue said. "This is where we are going to kick your ass."

"What are you planning?" Nina whispered to him. The three others weren't aware of what he was thinking, but he was hoping that they could use that to their advantage. If they didn't seem to have a strategy, then Mr. Trajan might think that they really were going to be easy to beat.

"Just trust me," Purdue said. He took a few steps forward toward Mr. Trajan. "Look at you, you big dumb bastard! All you are good for is doing the Visionaries' dirty work. You are just a big obedient dog, aye? That can't be ideal. Tell me, do they remember to let you out to take a shit before bed, or do you start whining and barking at the door?"

Purdue knew how to push people's buttons, and from the looks of Trajan's posture changing, he had found the big red button that he was looking for. He needed to get that brute fired up, angry enough to make a very stupid mistake.

Purdue took a few steps back toward the edge of the roof, with the bay behind him. The others followed his lead. They stood shoulder to shoulder in a line as Mr. Trajan looked ready to pounce and attack. The big masked man just needed one more little push to really set him off.

"You really are so disappointing! All of that talk and bluster about ripping us apart, and you can't even do that! We nearly had your sorry ass down in that corridor. You would have been stuck there for the rest of your life. You just got lucky...but besides that, you're not good for much, are you? The Visionaries probably just use you to carry things around, eh? That's all you are good for."

Mr. Trajan let out a roar and sprinted at them, charging like a bull—which was exactly what Purdue wanted. He could feel his friends getting nervous, knowing that they had nowhere to go as that lumbering beast of a man rushed toward them.

"Hold..." Purdue said. "Hold..."

Just as he was upon them, focusing on the one that had been mocking him, Purdue leaped out of the way to his right, rolling away and out of the man's path. Mr. Trajan couldn't stop his own charge in time and went stumbling over the end of the rooftop, plummeting down into the shores of the Mediterranean Sea below. They all watched as he crashed into the water. From that height, the collision with the water itself would have hurt, but with how rocky those shores were, it would have hurt even more.

"*That* was your plan?" Nina smacked him on the side of the head. "Lure him into the ocean while we all stood there like bowling pins?"

"It worked, didn't it?" Purdue countered. "Now come on. We need to get to the beach."

As they made their way down, he elaborated on his plan. "I don't care how big and strong Mr. Trajan is. He's still nowhere near as big or strong as the ocean. That drop was going to hurt no matter what too. It was the only thing I could think of that was going to do some real damage to the big bastard."

"It saved our lives," Callie said. "So it wasn't the worst idea."

"Thanks."

They made it down to the shore, where they found the enormous criminal washed up in the shallows. He had an injured leg that looked like it had been scraped against the rocky shore. There was some red water around where his injury was, but no one exactly had sympathy for him. He was soaked from head to toe and wasn't moving.

"Is he dead?" Nina asked.

Purdue carefully nudged the man with his foot, just praying that the giant wasn't going to suddenly spring awake and drag him into the sand with him. Luckily, he seemed like he was too injured to do anything like that. Purdue checked his pulse just to be safe but was horrified the whole time that Mr. Trajan was going to wake up.

"He's not dead," Purdue confirmed. "Seems he's just unconscious."

"That's better than rampaging around trying to beat us to death," Callie conceded. "So what now?"

"We take him hostage and have ourselves a chat with him. Elijah, help me lift him up, and let's get him out of here."

When the two men bent over to try to pick up the enormous man, Purdue's fear came true. Mr. Trajan suddenly regained consciousness and yelled out. He swung his fists wildly around from where he lay. Any one of those swings would have been enough to knock someone out if they made contact, but Purdue was careful to avoid them before throwing a punch of his own to the side of the giant's head. Mr. Trajan was too rattled and disoriented to defend himself, and Purdue's knuckle cracked against him, sending him back to a state of unconsciousness.

"Do you think he's actually going to cooperate?" Callie asked.

Purdue could only shrug. "I hope so."

∼

THE MAN WITH NO FUTURE

"You aren't ever going to amount to anything."

That was what his parents used to tell him, but he never cared much about what they had to say. He towered over both of them and knew that his anger frightened them. They just spoke down to him because they thought their parental authority gave them power over him; in some ways, it did, but that was all they had. When it came to physical strength, Andre wasn't afraid of anyone.

He had always been larger than the people around him, even growing up. He was twice the size of people his age and twice as tough too. He naturally liked to use his size to his advantage, like any kid would if they were given such natural strength. Still, he got into more fights than he probably should have, and all of the adults in his life looked at him with pity.

That was why his parents thought he would amount to nothing.

"Where do you see yourself in the future, Andre?" his mother asked him once. "What do you think is going to happen to you?"

"I don't know," he had said honestly. "Should I?"

"You're a young man now. You should at least be thinking about what you are going to do with your life."

The truth was, at the time, he had no idea what he wanted to do with his life. He didn't have many skill sets outside of being able to lift heavy things. He wasn't passionate about many things, and he didn't have a support system to help him navigate through any of them. His parents didn't believe in him, he couldn't make friends because everyone was so intimidated by him, and he wished he could do something useful with all of that strength. His future was looking so bleak.

Andre needed help, someone to help show him the right path to take, or at least one that would help him to make something of himself. He didn't want to prove his parents right. He wanted to be successful—*needed* to be successful.

That was when a voice had come to him, brilliant and wise, right through the speakers of his radio. It was a rich and powerful woman named Eve Wayneright, and she had so many ideas about the future. Everything she said made sense to Andre. He didn't have any issues with any of her opinions, to the point that it almost felt like they were sharing the same brain.

She talked about the future and what it could mean. She talked about unity. She talked about peace. She talked about serenity. The only problem was that all of the things she talked about were from a future she described and were not reality, but she had her own way of pulling the listeners into the future she envisioned. It felt so real and so perfect.

"The only thing holding us back..." Eve Wayneright's voice sounded so soothing through the radio. The words seeped into his ears and stuck themselves to his very soul. "...is our past. We, as a species, are obsessed with the past. We are beholden to it, tethered to it, and we can't move forward until those chains are severed. Get rid of what you don't need. Get rid of the things that only offer sentimental value. You don't need it. You don't need any of it. Once you do that, you will finally have room to breathe and room for an actual future to be whatever you want."

It was everything that Andre ever wanted to hear. It was someone that actually believed that he could be something someday, that his future wasn't so bleak and so hopeless. It gave him reason to want to try; it gave him reason to want to live.

From that point on, he listened to Eve Wayneright's speeches religiously. He absorbed every moment of her seminars and fought online against the people that doubted her words, the ones that claimed that she was some kind of charlatan or fraud. They didn't understand how helpful and inspirational she was. They didn't understand how she could change people's lives, just like she had changed his for the better.

He was a loyal subscriber and follower, joining all kinds of message boards and forums for like-minded individuals. He always spoke his mind in those kinds of places, unafraid to show his true beliefs, since he knew that the other people that frequented those places thought about things in a similar manner. They were all a collective of people who shared viewpoints on the world and what they wanted the future to be. He was part of something, constantly being motivated by others that saw more hopeful days ahead. It was wonderful.

Being a part of something like that helped motivate him to get into better shape because they constantly talked about how people would need to be stronger in the years to come to help protect the future that the rest of the world thought could never come.

That was when he received a text message from an unknown number:

We need you to help build and protect the future.

For days, that was all that he got, no matter how many responses he sent asking who the sender was or asking for them to elaborate. That one sentence sat on his phone, constantly poking at his mind with all kinds of theories. He wanted to know who the sender was, but no matter how much he begged for that answer, one didn't come.

Then a second text message arrived, just as simple—if not more so—than the first:

We need your strength in the days ahead.

Once again, Andre couldn't stop asking the sender to reveal themselves or explain what they meant by their cryptic messages, and once again, there were no responses or messages back from the ones that were messaging him.

It had to be some kind of trick, something to just toy with him and get his hopes up that he was meant for something more than the life that he lived. He couldn't stand it. In a fit of uncontrollable rage, he smashed his phone into pieces on his kitchen table, determined to stop those people messaging him from ever being able to send him anything again.

After buying his new phone, he at least felt like he was safe from any mysterious messages...but he was wrong.

The phone dinged in the middle of the night, waking him up. Through the haze of his sleepiness, he stared at the words on the phone's screen:

You must help us. You were chosen because you are strong and you are loyal. You are exactly who we need to fight for us.

- **The Visionaries**

He couldn't believe his eyes. At first, he doubted it was real, but the more he thought about it, the more it made sense. Who else would be sending him those messages? Who else would be able to track down his new phone after he destroyed the old one? Who else could possibly need his help in building a better future?

It was really the Visionaries, the people like Eve Wayneright, that wanted to provide a better future for the world. He was ready to help them take whatever the next steps were, to be part of the movement to make the world a better place.

Mr. Trajan sent a text back, but this one was not him begging for answers or pleading for them to reveal themselves. This time, he was hopefully sending them a message that they would acknowledge. He simply told them, "I'm in," and left it at that. How was he supposed to deny a request from the Visionaries? Whatever they needed help with, he was willing to do it. It wasn't every day that your heroes asked for your help.

The next series of texts was vague and cryptic, simply giving him instructions on where to meet. While he drove to the designated location, he tried to keep himself calm. There was still a chance that this was all some kind of elaborate prank, but deep down, he could feel that it was his future finally calling to him.

His parents were wrong. All of those kids he grew up with were wrong. His counselors were wrong. They all thought that he had no future and was not going to end up doing anything of any importance, and yet there he was, ready to save the world. Some day, those people that he couldn't stand might be forced to thank him. He would relish every second of that.

The first time that he met the two other people that were going to don the masks of the Third Triumvirate, he was not exactly impressed by them. They had their designated aliases and their masks, as well as their loyalty to the Visionaries. Besides that, Andre had nothing in common with the two people that he was supposed to work well with. They were two complete strangers that just so happened to want the same kind of future that he did.

They had no choice over who wore what mask or who took what name. All of that was already predesignated, and they were expected to respect that. Once they were settled in, they were shown footage of the group of thieves known as the Third Triumvirate, that wore similar masks to the ones they had on.

The tall, broad-shouldered, and muscular member, who had been called Mr. Commodus, reminded Andre of himself. It seemed like he was being put in as some sort of replacement for him or some kind of proxy. He was okay with that. He knew how to play to his strengths, especially when it was something that he really cared about.

When it came down to it, Andre was just happy that he had an important role to play in shaping the future. He knew that he was meant for more than most people believed.

Andre put the Mr. Trajan mask on for the first time, and the days ahead suddenly seemed so bright.

14

THE BREAKING POINT

It was not always easy to find a good place to interrogate someone. It needed to be someplace that they didn't recognize, and it needed to be someplace that would help to make them feel uncomfortable and unsafe. Most importantly, it needed to be someplace that was far away from any potential onlookers or anyone that would contact the police and interfere with the interrogation.

They were thankful that they found an abandoned warehouse not far from the fort. They spent the walk to that warehouse explaining to the people that their friend had been injured but was going to be okay as they all lugged the enormous man down sidewalks and across streets. When they finally got him to the warehouse, they tied him to a chair, making sure that he was restrained well enough that even his great strength wouldn't be able to break him out of it.

"You really think he is going to tell us anything?" Elijah asked. "I feel like men like that...they don't rat out their own people. He's not just going to spill his guts because we ask nicely."

"Who said anything about asking nicely," Callie said darkly. She moved toward the bound man, but Purdue caught her arm. She glanced down at it and shook her head. "What? I'm just going to make him talk. That's what we want?"

"And how exactly are you planning on making him talk, aye?"

"Going to beat some answers out of him. It's the least he and his friends deserve for wearing those masks."

"Listen, I can get excited about all kinds of things, and I usually don't have a problem with treading into gray areas, but we are not going to torture him."

"*You* don't have to."

"And you're not going to. We're just going to talk, that is all."

"If that is how you want to start it, that's fine. We get him comfortable, get him to feel safe, and then shatter that when I start prodding at him with a fire poker."

"I told you. We are not going to torture him."

Purdue wanted to get answers just as much as she did, but he didn't have that personal vendetta to settle like Callie did. While he was willing to do a lot of things to try to learn more about what they were looking for, he had no intention of letting someone be tortured to get what they wanted. That was taking things too far. He wouldn't cross that particular line.

"You are too close to this, Callie," Purdue said, realizing that it might have been a mistake to bring her with them. "Far too close. It's all about getting payback for these people impersonating the Third Triumvirate, aye? That's what this is really about."

"No, it's not, Purdue."

Purdue could see right through her. "Yes, it is. Go wait outside."

Callie didn't budge, and her face was growing red with anger. "You can't do—"

"I can," Purdue said firmly. "You are part of the Order of the Black Sun, and I am one of the leaders of the Order of the Black Sun. Asking you to wait outside is not a request that I am making. As your superior in our organization, I am giving you an order. And you will obey, aye?"

Purdue didn't like to force people to do things. He didn't like to wave his position and his power around to get what he wanted, but he had to nip this insubordination in the bud before Callie did something that would hurt their efforts. She was too angry about the new Third Triumvirate and too determined to make them pay for what they had done. They didn't need that right now.

They needed to focus on the breastplate of Alexander, not getting retribution.

Reluctantly, Callie stormed off and left the room. She was obviously livid, but it was for the best.

Purdue turned to Nina. "Can you make sure that she doesn't interfere?"

"Sure," Nina said and stood over by the door to ensure that Callie didn't come rushing back in to interrupt.

Purdue and Elijah approached the masked man, and Purdue knew exactly how he wanted to start the conversation. He put his hand on the stony visage of Trajan and then pried the mask off of their prisoner's face. The person underneath was scowling, glaring up at them with beady eyes and a ravenous expression, breathing heavily like a hungry beast.

Mr. Trajan growled, leering up at his captors. "So you caught me... What do you think is going to happen now? It is not going to be anything good for you, you know."

"We'll take our chances," Purdue said. "We just want to learn more about the whole operation of yours. The three of you decided to copy a group of criminals, stealing their entire aesthetic. Not very original of you."

"The Visionaries did that for you," Mr. Trajan said. "That's all. You think I give a shit about what that lady or her friends used to do? From what I heard, they were just a bunch of idiots trying to do something impossible. That's not exactly inspiring."

At least it was confirmed that the return of the Third Triumvirate—or at least, their imposters—was just a way for the Visionaries to try to toy with them. It was a psychological warfare tactic to make them feel like old enemies were coming back and that they couldn't actually get rid of their foes.

"I don't know for sure, but my guess is that we were all specifically chosen because we bare enough of a resemblance to that old group. Miss Augustus looks a lot like your friend, doesn't she?"

That was true, considering that just the sight of Miss Augustus initially made them all suspect that Callie might have fallen back to her old criminal ways. There was no denying that, with that mask on at least, they looked similar.

"And me...with my build, I think they wanted to swap me in for that big one that used to run with the Third Triumvirate."

"Mr. Commodus!" Callie's voice rang from the hall. She might have been out of the room, but she was clearly still interested in what was happening inside, listening in to the conversation. "His name was Mr. Commodus!"

Mr. Trajan just started cackling. "Yeah, him. That guy. They just wanted me for my strength, and that's fine by me. It's always been what I'm best at. My whole life, I've just been able to lift things up or move things that other people couldn't."

The man suddenly flexed and tried to break free from the restraints keeping him bound to the chair. For a second, it seemed like he was going to burst right out of his imprisonment. Purdue and Elijah flinched at the sudden outburst and waited for him to break free. Thankfully, he couldn't quite get out of the restraints. When he couldn't, he just kept laughing, shaking his head.

"Look at how scared you two look. What if I had gotten out? Would you have just stood there and let me beat you to death? Probably. You're obviously not prepared if that were to happen."

"We would figure out a way to manage," Purdue said, trying to regain his composure and not look too startled. "Tell us more about the Visionaries and their plans."

Mr. Trajan snorted and spat on the floor, grinning. "You really think it would just be that easy? You just ask me and I will start spilling all of the beans about them? That's not how this works. I believe in the future that they are making, and no part of that future includes me betraying them to you."

"And what have they done to guarantee such loyalty?" Purdue said. "From what I've seen, they are a bunch of rich egomaniacs obsessed with controlling the world. Why just be their puppet?"

"You really don't get it," Mr. Trajan said. "And I don't want to have to explain it to you."

"Humor us, then," Elijah said. "Because I don't understand it either. Why are you so devoted to them?"

Mr. Trajan rolled his eyes. "You obviously have never believed in anything...*really* believed in something. The three of us all listened to their teachings, and we all saw the painting they were trying to create on the canvas in our minds. Who wouldn't want to be part of creating a better future for the world?"

"So you were all fans and followers," Purdue surmised. "That's one thing, but when you take it to this kind of level...that's more than just being a supporter. You are nothing more than their stooge for obeying everything they say. You're brainwashed, mate. That's all."

"I am not brainwashed!" Mr. Trajan roared. "You all are just blind! You are content with this shit world as it is right now in the present, clouded by all of the bullshit that you can't see what could be instead! You don't see that it doesn't have to be this way!"

Despite what he claimed, the man definitely sounded more than a little brainwashed. Everything he said sounded like it was coming from someone else, from some kind of disturbed philosophy. It sounded like reality had been replaced by some radicalized fantasy.

"You don't think it's wrong to destroy pieces of history?" Elijah asked, leaning forward threateningly. "You don't see anything wrong with that? Nothing at all? Those are priceless and important things that shouldn't be ruined."

"According to you, maybe. But as for me? I don't give a damn one way or the other about what happens to some old piece of junk."

Elijah suddenly backhanded him, striking him hard in the face. Mr. Trajan just kept smiling, but the curator looked surprised by his own sudden outburst. He wasn't usually a violent person, but having his life's passion be insulted like that apparently could get a rise out of him.

"Elijah," Purdue said firmly, "don't force me to make you go stand out with Callie."

"I'm sorry...it's just...this man is trash, Purdue."

"I'm trash? The things that you all are so obsessed with collecting are the real pieces of trash! What's preserving them going to do? How do any of them help the world, hmm? It is all just clutter!"

Elijah raised his hand to strike him again but stopped himself from following through. He regained his composure and adjusted his glasses, turning to Purdue. "I am inclined to think that Callie was right that we are going about this the wrong way. This guy isn't going to tell us anything that we can use unless we pry it out of him."

While Elijah could be right, he had also just gotten upset and might have just been talking out of a place of anger. Acting emotionally wasn't how they should be making their decisions. Purdue was still hesitant, but as he looked at their captive, it was obvious that the current discussion wasn't going to get them anywhere.

Mr. Trajan didn't seem too intimidated by their talk of torture, though. He licked his lips and goaded them. "Come on then! Do your worst. You bookworms won't be able to do shit to me."

While Purdue didn't want to have to torture the man, the fact that he was welcoming it and challenging them made Purdue feel a little less bad about having to go through with it. He waved for Nina to let Callie in. When Callie returned, she was staring at Mr. Trajan and never averted her gaze as she approached.

Everyone got out of her way, stepping back while she slowly walked over to their prisoner. It had taken them all a while to see the good in her and to stop seeing her as some kind of villain; suddenly, they had forgotten all of that progress, and all felt the intimidation that she used to bring when they first met her as Miss Caligula. She carried herself differently—she was much scarier.

"Tell us everything you know about the Visionaries," she said coldly. "Now."

Mr. Trajan shook his head. "I told you all already. I have no intention of doing anything that would put their future at risk. I am not going to do it. Do your worst, girlie."

Callie's lips curled into a twisted smile. It was scary to see her that way. Her entire posture had changed. She wasn't the young woman that had done everything she could to clear her name and become trusted. She wasn't the kindhearted person that was just trying to get people to stop judging her. She wasn't the woman that had been excited to try to go after the breastplate of Alexander. She was the vengeful, scorned Miss Caligula, looking to enact vengeance on someone that had tarnished her legacy and mocked her past.

"Oh, I plan to." Callie glanced back at the others. "You may not want to be here for this."

It wasn't a command to leave like Purdue had given her. It was a warning that they may not be able to handle whatever was about to happen. That was nerve-racking, but he couldn't help but be a little bit curious about it too.

Callie picked up a piece of debris inside of the room, just a piece of concrete that had fallen off of the wall over time, and immediately struck Mr. Trajan in the side of the head with it. It seemed to be a bit harder of a blow than he was expecting as he let out a roar of pain followed by a long list of profanities, screaming at the top of his lungs at the woman that had begun her torture.

"What the hell do you think you're doing!?"

Callie didn't answer. She just hit him again in the exact same spot without a word. It seemed like she hit him even harder that time and his whole enormous body was reverberating from the blow. He writhed in the chair, trying to break free of the restraints as a line of blood dripped down the side of his head from a new welt that had formed.

"You crazy bitch!" Mr. Trajan spat. "You can't just—"

The piece of debris clocked him in the skull in the identical spot yet again, making his head wobble on his shoulders. His muscles pulsated violently as he tried desperately to break free of the bindings around his wrists. He wanted to get free from the chair to throttle the woman that was clearly causing him a lot of pain. He was more than angry; he was the kind of furious that you only got when your life was in danger and you were scared that you were about to lose it.

Purdue was surprised by Callie's extremely direct approach to torturing him. She didn't do it with any kind of finesse or grace. She didn't slowly cut into him or peel away at him—at least not yet. Actually, as Purdue thought of it, he realized that the blunt force trauma she was causing Mr. Trajan was just the opening salvos, a way to get his mind to realize that he shouldn't be so comfortable.

Callie held the piece of debris in front of his face, showing him the specks of blood that were now on it that had come from his cranium. She wanted him to see what she was doing to him, the start of the pain that she was going to inflict. It was the best way to start to bring down someone of his stature; she had to prove to him that she was going to break him down little by little until he wasn't the towering goliath anymore.

Mr. Trajan cracked his neck and shook his head like he was trying to knock the wound off of his head. "You are going to have to do a hell of a lot better than that if you want to—"

Callie hit him again and then again.

The thief let out a loud groan of pain, staring at the floor. He must have been seeing stars after those hits. She was knocking the defiance out of him with those blows, hitting him hard enough for him to ignore his perceived strength and endurance.

"You...I am going to pull your head off for this..."

"Worry about your own head," Callie said and hit him one more time with the shard of stone before letting it drop to the floor beside them. She grabbed Mr. Trajan by his hair and pulled his head up so that he was facing her. "You know, you looked a lot better with the mask on. That fake Third Triumvirate mask. You really didn't feel like a fraud with that on? You should have. You were just posing, pretending to be something that you were not. That could not have been very satisfying for you. There is really no dignity in doing something like that, is there?"

"You wouldn't get it." Mr. Trajan looked like he was about to pass out from all of those hits to his head. Still, he glowered at his torturer and tried to keep his head up. "You never gave a shit about the future, probably. It's just this vague idea that you assume will always be there. You take it for granted, just like everyone else. This world is rotting, and it will take time and effort to reverse what's happening to it. The only people that are looking that far ahead are the Visionaries."

"See?" Callie said, smirking. "Now you are telling me something useful. So is it really so hard not to tell me just a little bit more? Who are the rest of their members? Where are they hiding? Do they have any particular weaknesses that we can exploit? These are the kinds of questions that I really, really need answered, Mr. Trajan. So just be a good boy and tell us what we want to know. If you don't, I'm going to continue, and it's not going to just be hitting you in the head."

Nina leaned over to Purdue. "She really can be scary. I forgot how she could get like this. When we first met and she was, well, trying to kill me, this was how she acted back then. This was the girl that I saw, the one that made me fear for my life."

"It's nice that she's on our side now, aye?" Purdue snickered. It really was a blessing that she was no longer an enemy. She was absolutely terrifying to the people that she did not like.

"I'm not telling you shit," the large man grumbled. "Not a goddamn thing. None of you. You don't deserve to know about any of the things that we have planned for this world. We are going to make sure that you don't make it that long so it doesn't concern you anyway."

"Don't you think it's concerning?" Callie asked, slapping his face. "Aren't you nervous that you are just going along with all of these people and all of their big ideas, just a pawn that they probably think is expendable?"

"They don't think we're expendable. They treat everyone that follows them with respect. They see us as people that are visionaries just like them because we can see the same thing that they see."

"The same delusions, you mean," Purdue chimed in but was quieted by a glare from Callie. She obviously wanted Mr. Trajan to feel like he was isolated with her.

Callie continued. "I know it must be comforting to think that, but I think it's pretty obvious that that is not the case. Even from just what we've seen of the Visionaries, they are rich and powerful people, influential types that don't care about the little people unless those little people can do something for them. I know you are a big, tall, strong man, but you are one of those little people to them, Mr. Trajan. You and the rest of this new Third Triumvirate were just gullible enough to throw on those masks and do whatever you were told."

"You're wrong," Mr. Trajan snarled. "It was an honor reserved only for the most loyal."

"You obviously want to be special, but you are not special to them. You don't think that they can replace you? You don't think that they would? I promise you, you are irreplaceable. If anything happened to you, they would just find the next biggest guy that believed in their garbage, and they would put the mask on him. Maybe it would be the same mask or maybe they would give him a different emperor. Whatever the case, you would be forgotten long before they create that perfect future you keep talking about."

Callie pulled out a switchblade and showed the knife to Mr. Trajan.

"Oh, you are going to cut me now? How original! Blunt force isn't enough...have to bring the sharp things into it."

"I'm not going to cut you," Callie said coldly. She turned to her allies. "This is the part when you might really want to leave."

Elijah didn't hesitate to walk out the door. He didn't have an appetite to see someone get tortured more. Nina moved to leave, too, but stopped when she noticed that Purdue was not budging from where he stood. She took him by the arm to help try to guide him out, but he had no intention of leaving. He needed to see what she would do next.

He very quickly wished that he hadn't stayed when Callie slid the blade underneath the fingernail of Mr. Trajan's right index finger. The criminal's expression completely shifted. His mouth fell open, and his eyes grew wide with surprise—and, most of all, fear.

"What are you doing?"

"Prying your fingernails off like I said I would," Callie said. "I would say that this won't hurt, but it's really, *really* going to hurt."

With a flick of her wrist, she tore the nail right off the tip of the finger. Mr. Trajan cried out in more pain than he had shown so far. It seemed so much worse than those hard hits with that rock earlier. This was more than just battering away at him. This was picking him apart. He flailed around wildly in the chair, wheezing and swearing. The blood where his fingernail used to be was a reminder of what used to be. Purdue didn't know how long it would take for a fingernail to grow back, but he couldn't imagine losing his nail completely like that.

Watching Callie perform that kind of torture sent a shiver down his spine. He couldn't help but wonder how experienced she was in causing people harm like that. She seemed to know what she was doing. How many people had she already done similar things to back when she was Miss Caligula? How many victims had lost their fingernails while staring into the passive expression of that mask she used to wear?

"Please. Please don't."

"Oh, come on," Callie said with a wicked grin. "You had a chance to talk earlier without any of this, and you were so sure that you didn't want to. You refused over and over again. But now, just when we're getting started—when I am just starting to have some real fun—you want to start begging for mercy? That's just unbecoming."

She ignored his pleas and ripped off another nail, making him howl in agony once again. It was becoming hard to tell if Callie was just playing up the sadistic act to scare him or if she was really enjoying causing him pain. It was hard to deny that joyful glint in her eye each time she slid the blade under the nail. Most people didn't look so happy when they found themselves in a position where they had to torture another human being. It was incredibly unsettling to witness, but Purdue was not nearly as unsettled by it as Mr. Trajan probably was.

"Tell us what you know about the Visionaries! Now!"

The behemoth finally had had enough. He let out a loud cry. "Okay! Okay! Just stop! Just stop! I'll tell you what I know! I'll tell you..."

Callie kept that blade firmly under the next nail threateningly. "And I don't want you to be making up any bullshit with your answers."

"I won't...I swear I won't...please."

Purdue was inclined to believe him. Everyone had their breaking point. There was only so much that he could take, even someone as formidable as him.

Callie wasn't quite as convinced clearly as she immediately tore off the next nail, sending the man into a sobbing bout of hysterics. He didn't even have the strength to try to break free anymore. His resistance had been completely demolished by her blade.

It was surprising to see that she was still going but then she stepped back and didn't slip the knife under the next nail. It seemed that she just wanted to give him one last example of pain, a reminder of what she could do to him if she wanted.

"You don't get to dictate when this stops," Callie said. "But you better start talking right now."

The woman in front of Purdue was merciless, ruthless, and borderline sadistic, and he was suddenly so much more afraid of her than he ever had been before. It was strange to think that it was the same woman that he was laughing with, that helped them out so often, and that was so self-conscious about her place as a member of the Order of the Black Sun. She was so different in that moment, so powerful.

"I don't know all that much about the Visionaries themselves, alright? It was never about that. It was never about turning them into celebrities. They didn't want that. They just wanted to spread the message to the people that were willing to hear them."

"People like you and the other Third Triumvirate imposters," Purdue surmised.

"We could see what they were talking about and how they wanted to fix the world, yeah. All we wanted to do was make those dreams...that future...a reality. That's it. They have the means to do it, and they are going to. The rest of the world just needs to get on board. It's inevitable at this point."

"You think that the world should join in on setting fire to museums, destroying monuments, and desecrating burial sites?" Nina asked, fuming. "You are actually going to tell me that you *really* believe that?"

Mr. Trajan shrugged. "I do. I have never understood what keeping all of that junk around really did. How does it help anyone? We spend so much money on museums and landmarks and history books, things that don't matter to what is happening in the world now. Why is the world so obsessed with holding on to those things?"

"Ever since we found out about the Visionaries, we have been hearing that same shit over and over again," Purdue said. "Eventually, it all just becomes white noise, and it's pretty damn clear that you all have been brainwashed by that noise. It's you all that have been fed the same talking points and forgot how to have any coherent thoughts of your own."

Mr. Trajan glared up at them. It seemed that the submissiveness that the torture had brought was starting to wear off. Callie stepped closer just to remind him that he was still under duress.

"Keep talking," she said. "About the Visionaries themselves. Not their seminars."

"I told you. I don't know much about the actual people running thing—"

"Then tell us something you do know!" Callie slid her little blade underneath one of his remaining fingernails and they all watched as absolute fear moved through the man's large body, practically petrifying him where he sat. He stared down at his finger nervously, grinding his teeth.

"Look...you want to find the armor that Alexander wore, right? That one that they say keeps the person wearing it safe?"

"Obviously," Elijah said. "That's why we are out here to begin with. To stop people like you from getting it and ruining it. Unlike you and your buddies, we actually care about what happened before us."

"Why?" Mr. Trajan snorted. "None of that matters. Haven't you ever heard to let the past be the past and focus on the here and now? Or better yet, focus on where you want to be going. Don't trip on something behind you."

Nina rolled her eyes. "You sound like a really bad fortune cookie. They really drilled all of this nonsense into your head, huh?"

"I'll be drilling this knife into his head if he doesn't start saying something worthwhile," Callie said darkly. She really had leaned into her darker tendencies when given the opportunity. It was a little bit scary.

Their captive seemed hesitant to divulge anything specific. No matter how much he wanted the torture to stop, his loyalty to the Visionaries and his allies was still very strong. He really didn't want to give them anything that would put the Visionaries or their mission at risk.

Callie put the blade up to his neck.

"Talk, or I'm going to start pulling teeth out."

Reluctantly, he spoke and looked very defeated when he did. "They were talking about a vault. A secret place where Caligula put a lot of his most prized possessions. That was where we were going to go next after Miss

Augustus got that call. That is where the breastplate probably is!"

That was at least something—much more than he had given them up until that point.

Callie stared down at him and offered a very strange smile. "The location of this vault. Now."

Mr. Trajan initially seemed resistant but, after a few seconds of contemplation, gave in. He must have realized that the pain would continue if he didn't continue to play along. He had to cooperate or she was going to start pulling him apart again. Slowly, he told them the coordinates before leaning back in the chair, exhausted.

"That's all she told me...it's all I know, okay? I'm supposed to meet them there."

"Thank you," Callie said. "You have been so cooperative."

Without another word, Callie slid the blade beneath one of the last remaining nails and ripped it off. Mr. Trajan cried out in a familiar shriek, swearing and cussing her out. "I told you everything! I told you everything!"

"That was just one last one for the road," Callie said before punching him in the face and knocking him unconscious in his seat.

Everyone watched as she brushed herself off and walked over to them like everything was perfectly normal. Callie didn't seem overly bothered by everything that had happened. Purdue felt drained just from having witnessed all of it. That was nothing compared to how hands-on she had been with all that torture. He would have thought that she would have at least needed to rest or something, but she seemed perfectly normal.

"Are you alright?" Purdue couldn't help but ask.

"I'm good," Callie said. "It wasn't easy, but it was nothing new for me, unfortunately. Still, it had to be done, so I got it done. And I have to admit, it was just a little satisfying that I got to make someone like him beg for mercy. That is not something that happens very often. When would I usually get the opportunity to torture a guy that has tried to humiliate me? It was an opportunity that could not be passed up."

Callie's torture session had undeniably gotten them results, and sometimes that mattered more than the actual methods. The way she had tortured him might have been scary, but if it worked, that didn't matter as much.

"Was it difficult for you?"

"What do you mean?" Callie asked. "The torture part wasn't hard. I was just a little bit rusty."

"Not the torturing necessarily...more the getting back into that mode. You seemed like a completely different person in that room."

"Oh yeah...that was difficult to tap into. I'll admit. It's like...I was like that once, you know? I would do those things and not think twice about it. I felt like a completely different person, and in some ways, Miss Caligula is not me. I had to find a little piece of her and use the things that I knew back then, that I haven't had any reason to use in a long time."

"How did it feel?"

Callie frowned. "Not great, to be honest. That's part of me that I would really prefer to leave in the past, but I guess some things just can't stay buried, can they?"

"Unfortunately not."

"Don't worry about me. It was just a temporary situation. I don't plan on digging up any more of that anytime soon."

"That's good to hear," Purdue said.

"You're not scared of me now, are you?"

Purdue put his trembling hand in his pocket but winked at her. "Aye. Maybe a little."

∽

Nina and Elijah stood outside of the warehouse, just trying to get some air after everything that they had seen. Nina was struggling with some of the things that she had just observed. As much as she appreciated Callie and was happy to have her on their side, seeing that side of her again stirred up some unpleasant memories from when they had been enemies.

"That was...unpleasant, wasn't it?" Elijah asked, cleaning off his glasses like he was trying to wipe away what those lenses had seen in their reflection. "I didn't know she still had all of that in her."

"Neither did I," Nina said. "That's what she used to be like. She was so ruthless. She didn't care at all about who she hurt or why she did it. It was weird to see her like that again. That was the Miss Caligula I knew, the one that I used to have nightmares about."

"I think Mr. Trajan is going to have nightmares about her too after today," Elijah said. "I don't think we have anything to worry about with her. I think all we can do is just appreciate that she is no longer our enemy and now she is on our side. I would much rather have her as a friend than as a foe after that."

"That's true," Nina said. "And it wasn't like she tapped into that side of her for no reason. She managed to get us something good out of all of that."

"The location of Caligula's secret vault..." Elijah looked like he was suddenly filled with so much energy and anticipation. "I can't wait to see it. We need to leave immediately, though, if we want to have any chance of beating Miss Augustus to it."

"Agreed," Nina said. "Let's get the others."

15

WITHOUT A THIRD

Miss Augustus was not overly bothered by the loss of Mr. Trajan, and she didn't even try to hide it. He was an aggressive brute that forced his opinion into every conversation, trying to dominate every choice that they made, at least when it came to their group of three. Luckily, he shared their loyalty to the Visionaries, so he would follow their commands, but it was always difficult when it came to following hers, despite the fact that the group that they served specifically chose her to lead the new iteration of the Third Triumvirate. It was at least a lot quieter without him around.

"You don't think that he would actually turn on us, do you?" Mr. Aurelius asked nervously.

Mr. Aurelius—who she knew before all of this, before the masks, as a man named Devin Roy—was a meek and timid individual that only decided to start showing any hints of purpose once he hid his own face behind that mask. Still, the mask couldn't hide the truth from someone that knew him beforehand. She saw right through the face of Marcus Aurelius that he had on, right to what kind of person he actually was. His book smarts were why he was useful; he was only there to help pour over useful information. He wasn't a great companion to have, but he was at least less hostile than Mr. Trajan was.

"I doubt it," she said. "That oaf might be dumb, but I don't think that he would say anything that would do damage to the Visionaries' plans. He wouldn't dare."

"I hope you're right," Devin Roy said, rubbing his hands together nervously. "He just strikes me as the kind of guy that would say whatever he had to if it meant saving his own skin."

"It doesn't matter," she said, sure that her remaining companion was just nervous. "Even if he tells them something, we have the head start. We have an idea of where Caligula's vault is. And if he tells them, that's fine. We'll be lying in wait for them."

"Should we worry about setting a trap? I thought we weren't supposed to do anything to them ourselves? We should just find that breastplate and get out of there as quickly as possible. That's what I say."

"Oh, Devin..." She enjoyed using his real name when she spoke to him. It made it clear that she did not respect this new identity he had made for himself and knew exactly who he was, mask or not. It was a reminder that the mask didn't really change anything if she knew who was behind it. "Yes, we have orders not to take them out, but that doesn't mean that we can't. If anything, maybe getting rid of the Visionaries' enemies is exactly what they want us to do."

"I don't think so," Devin Roy said. "They seemed quite clear with the instructions."

"Look. You have your head buried in your history books and in all of the things we need to know about Caligula. I'll focus on the here and now."

For someone that was a follower of the Visionaries, a group that wanted to destroy the obsession with history and the past, she was surprised that a historian like Devin Roy was part of their cause. Most historians didn't want to hear about any of the philosophies that they lived by. They thought that what they were doing was an absolute sacrilege of everything that they believed in.

She supposed there was no better time to ask him about it than then, considering they no longer had a huge ox of a man with them during every conversation. They finally had a chance to speak alone.

"Why did you take such an interest in the Visionaries, Devin?" she asked bluntly. "I've never asked, but I've always wondered... It just doesn't seem like something you would want to do, given your occupation."

Mr. Aurelius gave one of his usual nervous little laughs. "I guess it does seem a little peculiar, doesn't it? Like I'm betraying history itself or something. The truth is, I've always just been good at remembering dates and events and things like that. It was just what I was best at, so leaning into that as my job just seemed like a natural fit. Do I care if we keep harping on about the same things over and over again? Not really, no. I don't think that it would be a great loss to destroy every single history textbook in the world. There are only so many times that we can keep regurgitating the same redundant information time and time again, you know?"

She supposed that she understood that. It still seemed strange, but he had been a devout follower. She didn't think that he was trying to do anything underhanded. "So when we burn those scrolls or smash those vases to pieces...none of that bothers you?"

"No. All of those are just material things that really don't need to still be around. History was at its most effective when it was told through stories, through oral means, where we could learn from the things that happened before. Holding on to those kinds of things just takes up unnecessary space. I'll be glad when they are all gone."

It felt good to reaffirm his commitment to the cause now that it was just the two of them. As far as she was concerned, Mr. Trajan was a lost cause and it was up to them to finish the task that they had been given by the Visionaries to find that breastplate and make sure that it was destroyed.

"You really think that the Visionaries would appreciate us being the ones to take out those people?"

"In the long run, how upset will they be with us for helping them?" she asked. "After how much they are continuing to be a problem, I don't think that they will mind all that much, honestly. They might even reward us."

That seemed to excite him. He wanted to be noticed. He wanted to be appreciated, especially by the Visionaries. At least he would listen to her more than Mr. Trajan would. They may have been down one member of their triumvirate, but they might do better without him slowing them down.

Now they just had to get to that secret vault of Caligula's. They could figure out the rest from there.

16

THE WAIT

Damon Meyer sat at his computer monitor, with his phone beside him, waiting for some kind of update from the trio of followers whom he had given those Third Triumvirate masks. All three of those individuals had been vetted and reviewed, chosen because they were hardworking and very loyal to the Visionary cause. They seemed like they would be reliable. That was what mattered most. The three of them had been entrusted with not only destroying something that belonged to Alexander the Great but also providing more information on David Purdue and the Order of the Black Sun.

Some words appeared on the computer monitor in front of him, where the other remaining members of the Visionaries were also anxiously awaiting a report from their followers.

Anything?

"Nothing yet," Damon said calmly. The only downside to preferring to speak vocally over typing was that he couldn't mask his emotions as easily as the others could. He didn't want them to hear his nervousness or his disappointment. But that was his own fault for wanting to be heard. "I'm confident that Miss Augustus will fill us in on what is happening very soon. She is very devoted to our cause. She wouldn't do anything underhanded."

Let us hope not.

That would be unfortunate.

"I assure you, my friends, that everything is under control and we have nothing to worry about. Soon enough, Alexander's breastplate will be destroyed. That is one less piece of history littering the world, bringing us one small step closer to our ultimate goals."

How optimistic of you. When you first proposed that we focus on the threat that the Order of the Black Sun posed, we believed that you understood that they needed to be handled with tact. They are the greatest obstacles to our cause.

"Believe it or not, I am very aware of that. The way to break them was to hit them with psychological warfare, and that's what I've done. We'll see how it turns out."

Damon's phone suddenly started ringing, and when he picked it up, he heard the familiar voice of Miss Augustus on the other end. He made sure to mute his microphone so the other Visionaries would not be able to overhear the conversation that he was having with her.

"What is it?"

"We are on our way to Caligula's vault, but we did lose Mr. Trajan."

Damon couldn't believe what he was hearing. He wasn't sure if that meant that Mr. Trajan had died or if he was physically lost. It seemed unlikely that they would have lost such a goliath of a man.

"What do you mean you lost him?"

"I mean that he stayed behind back in Alexandria. He wanted to kill David Purdue and the other members of the Order of the Black Sun for you."

"I gave you all specific instructions to do otherwise."

"I know," Miss Augustus said. "I tried to tell him that but he thought that you would all be thankful that he got rid of them for you. He wouldn't listen to reason when I tried. So we left him behind. I don't know what happened after that. I told him the coordinates of where we are going to Caligula's vault."

Damon was infuriated but couldn't let her hear that. It wasn't Miss Augustus that he was most upset with. It was Mr. Trajan for not only defying the orders that he had been given but also becoming a potential liability by staying behind. Even if he did succeed in killing the Order of the Black Sun members, it didn't change the fact that he disobeyed and acted with insubordination. There would still be good reason to punish him.

"Don't go straight to Caligula's vault. Wait and see if Mr. Trajan makes contact or if the Order of the Black Sun gets there. If they have, then they no doubt managed to get the information out of that oaf."

"What then?"

"You will still try to complete your objective and destroy the breastplate of Alexander as planned."

Before she could say anything else, he hung up the phone. At the start of this exercise, he thought that "resurrecting" the Third Triumvirate would be a good way to put the Order of the Black Sun off balance, but now he saw how fruitless that had been. He should never have put so much faith in people that devoted their lives to following others.

If he wanted it done right, he would have to do it himself.

He turned the microphone back on to address his fellow Visionaries. "If anyone is looking for me, I will be going to Rome to ensure that the operation is finished properly."

The other Visionaries seemed amused by the news.

I do hope nothing is wrong.

It sounds like you are cleaning up a serious mess. Why else would you personally get involved?

This is why we do not put our resources into psychological warfare. Too much risk.

If he had stayed a moment longer, he probably would have yelled at all of them. Instead, he logged off his computer and immediately made ready to travel to the coordinates of Caligula's secret treasure trove.

It was time to make sure that things ended on a good note.

17

THE VAULT OF THE MAD EMPEROR

The coordinates that Mr. Trajan had given them ended up taking them all the way back to Italy, not far away from Rome. It was frustrating that they had been so much closer to it at the start of the journey than they were during their search in Alexandria, but Purdue knew that sometimes that was just what happened when you were searching the whole world for something. It was a risk of globetrotting without a clear destination. Sometimes you were taken far off course.

At least the curator had been in a much better mood ever since learning about Caligula's secret vault. Elijah had much more pep in his step, and he looked so excited—and he usually only looked that way when he was given a new relic to examine. He never looked that way while on a field mission, but he just couldn't help himself.

"Can you imagine what kind of items must be within that vault? Caligula had complete dominance over a whole empire. He must have collected all kinds of things. The possibilities are nearly endless."

Elijah was so thrilled by the prospect that he might be adding even more items to the Order of the Black Sun's deep vault than just the breastplate. That would be a nice added bonus to his personal wish list that had prompted the expedition to begin with.

"I wouldn't get too excited," Callie said. "Knowing the kinds of things that Caligula got up to, there might be some very disturbing things in his personal collection."

"Disturbing is fine as long as it is interesting," Elijah said. "I can handle some queasiness as long as it is something worth looking at."

"I don't know," Callie said. "He got up to some pretty revolting things. There are probably torture devices and ancient sex toys, considering the number of orgies he hosted."

While Elijah looked a little bit uncomfortable after that, he still maintained his initial stance. "Either way, I would rather see with my own eyes. Considering his position, there has to be something of value along with Alexander's armor as well. There has to be. And I cannot wait to get my hands on whatever there is."

Purdue wasn't going to try to dissuade him from his enthusiasm. It was so rare to see the curator be excited about anything. Elijah deserved to feel the thrill of the hunt, of being close to finding something he wanted.

That was what always made the expeditions so enjoyable.

The coordinates brought them to a mountain range near Rome but far away from where anyone resided. It was a good place to hide something and hopefully had never been found in the long period of time between Caligula's reign and the modern day. It would be very unfortunate if someone had already discovered it and raided it of its contents. Elijah's dream would be shattered and the curator would be absolutely devastated. With how refreshing it had been to see him looking so happy, Purdue wouldn't be able to take seeing that get ripped away. The curator would probably never come on a field expedition ever again if that ended up happening.

At first, it looked like there was nothing there. It was just a hilly, grass-covered landscape that didn't look remarkable whatsoever. If they had just given it a glance, they wouldn't have seen anything at all. That was probably what happened with most people, but Purdue couldn't help but notice that there was a slab of rock in the ground that seemed like it had been put there intentionally.

At least it seemed like Miss Augustus and Mr. Aurelius hadn't been there. If they had, they must have noticed that stone.

"Here, help me lift this."

The four of them all took a side of the slab of stone and heaved it up with all of their might, exposing a hole in the ground. It was impossible to see where the hole went, but it was the best lead that they had.

"So, who wants to take the dive?" Purdue asked. He really didn't want to be the first one in again. "I don't think it should be me. I bring bad luck when I lead. Remember last time in the fort? I led the way and all I found were those Third Triumvirate posers."

"That's true," Elijah said, stepping forward. "I will go. If this is where the breastplate is, I want to be the first one to see it. No offense."

That was fair. This was one of Elijah's dream expeditions, and the armor was one of the prizes that he most wanted to inspect. It practically belonged to him, and he had every right to be the first one to see it.

"Aye, that works for me."

The two ladies of the group agreed.

Elijah slowly lowered himself into the hole, though he looked a little bit nervous that it was impossible to see where it led. He was not quite used to that sense of exploration and that excitement that came from going somewhere that most people wouldn't dare to go. Still, Purdue felt some pride seeing himself go down into it when he was obviously nervous about where he would end up. Once the curator disappeared into the dark hole, they waited to hear some kind of update. After a minute, Elijah shouted up to them, his voice echoing out of the hidden hole.

"There's a chamber down here!"

That was all they needed to hear to follow. Nina went next, followed by Callie, but Purdue stood up on the grass for another minute. He looked around, scanning the area to try to make sure that they were not being watched. It seemed like the coast was clear but he couldn't ignore the hairs standing up on the back of his neck. They weren't the only ones with the coordinates for the location, after all.

Purdue reluctantly climbed down the hole until he was completely beneath the surface of the earth, joining his three companions underground. It was an old chamber built into the rock and stone around them. For how over the top and insane Caligula had been, his secret vault was rather low-key. He may have had garish parties and public executions, but he obviously wanted to keep his treasures hidden away.

Elijah's excitement was palpable beside him. "Here we go."

"I hope we find it," Purdue said, patting him on the back. "I hope *you* find it."

"Me too."

They stared at the contents within that hidden chamber and found things that most people probably would not consider treasure—but most people were not the infamous Caligula.

There was a pile of seashells stacked messily in one corner of the chamber, poured out onto the floor. Those seashells must have been sitting in that spot for thousands of years, dried up and so far from the sea where they originated. Nina and Callie both laughed when they approached the toppled stack of shells.

"You're kidding me," Nina said. "These must be the shells that he had the armies collect when he commanded them to go to the shoreline and start picking a fight with Neptune and the ocean itself. He told them to bring seashells back as trophies of their great victory, and it looks like they did just that."

"I'm not surprised," Callie said. "Caligula would be fixated on the strangest things. Like...that, for instance." Callie pointed to a strange four-legged silhouette at the other end of the chamber. It was a wooden horse that almost looked like some kind of effigy. "To commemorate his beloved steed, Incitatus. He might not have been able to give the horse the positions of power that he wanted, but it didn't stop him from trying. Personally, I think he would have made it a co-leader of the entirety of Rome if he could."

"Insanity..." Purdue said with an exhale.

Elijah Dane was just as unimpressed by their discovery. He rummaged through the pile of shells, nonchalantly tossing them over his shoulder to shatter. Purdue was surprised by the curator's lack of tact but it was obvious that he didn't even think of those shells as relics of any kind. That was rare for him and said a lot about how worthless those "trophies" really were.

After how excited he had been, it was hard to see the disappointment in Elijah's eyes. He took off his glasses and wiped them off before putting them back on his face like he was hoping he would find something more impressive once the lenses were clean.

"I expected better," Elijah said. "An emperor builds a secret vault for all of his treasures... I would have thought that he would have had something that was actually worth our time. The breastplate, for instance."

"Now, now," Purdue said. "We have barely started even searching. It still might very well be here."

"Or it very well might not," Elijah said with his usual pessimistic tone. He was obviously let down. He must have been expecting to find the breastplate at the center of the chamber, ready and waiting to be acquired. "Caligula seems like the kind of guy that might have just gotten rid of it."

"I doubt it," Callie said. "Obviously, he liked holding on to things. Just look at this place. A lot of these things don't have value in a traditional sense. It's obsessive, sentimental value. That's what he obviously cared about. He cared about the things that mattered to him on a personal level, like his horse or his pretend war against a god. If he cared enough to dig up the breastplate, then he probably would have held on to that too."

That was a fair point, and who knew more about Caligula than the woman that wore a replica of his face for some time? If Purdue trusted anyone to know best about what Caligula might have done, it was her.

All Purdue knew was that they needed to inspect every part of that chamber to be sure. Thoroughness sometimes offered better results than could be found in just the first few moments of finding something. He pushed aside his curator's negativity and focused on the task at hand—getting to that piece of armor before their enemies could.

There was a smaller chamber behind the first, deeper inside and further below the earth—a place that was obviously meant to be far away from prying eyes.

"Hopefully, these...items...in here are just meant to distract from this place," Elijah said optimistically, starting to perk up from his initial disappointment. "It almost worked on me. I was about ready to give up."

"And if it's more of the same?" Callie asked with a little laugh.

Elijah frowned. "I don't know if my heart would be able to handle that."

They all slowly—with a little bit of hope left—stepped into the second chamber. There were sarissa spears on the floor, so long that they nearly covered the whole length of the chamber. That was a good sign. That was one thing that came from Alexander the Great, so maybe there could be more. They stepped over those long spears and crept around toward the back of the chamber.

Purdue was starting to get worried. They were running out of chamber to search and still had not found the piece of armor. It would be devastating to have come to another dead end after the disappointment of Alexandria. For a moment, it looked like they really had found nothing again, but then Elijah called out.

"Here! In the corner!"

The curator lifted something up out of the darkness of the corner of the chamber and held it in the air. It was covered in dust and webs, but as he wiped it off, its appearance became easier to see. Sure enough, it looked like a breastplate.

"Is that the one?" Nina asked excitedly.

"It has to be!" Callie exclaimed, bursting with glee.

Purdue really hoped so, but he wasn't going to celebrate until Elijah confirmed it. The curator looked it over carefully, inspecting every minor detail to try to decipher its age and origin. He couldn't hide the smile that started to form on his face, though, as his eyes grew wide with excitement behind his glasses.

"Undeniably Macedonian. This is it. It has to be."

They all erupted in celebration, so relieved to have gotten to it before their enemies. Purdue pulled Elijah into a big hug, even though it obviously made the curator a little bit uncomfortable. He had told him that he was going to help get something from his wish list, and now he was holding it in his hands. It was an unbelievable feeling of accomplishment for Purdue, so he couldn't imagine how good it must have felt for Elijah to finally have the armor in his possession.

"We did it, guys," Callie said with a sigh of relief. "I really wasn't sure there for a minute. We cleared my name. We got the breastplate of Alexander. We beat at least one of the imposters. Things turned out pretty well, I'd say."

"I don't know about that," a voice said from behind them. "Don't speak too soon."

They all swung around to find the source of the words and found two masked figures looking back at them.

"Here you all are." Miss Augustus stepped into the chamber. "I really thought that we were going to beat you to it but it looks like you had a second wind. Was it Mr. Trajan? Did he mess this up for us?"

"Yeah, he squealed like a pig," Elijah said darkly, wanting to rub it in that they got to the breastplate before the Triumvirate did. "And he could see which side was going to end up getting it in the end."

"I doubt that," Miss Augustus said. "Trajan knew just like we do that the Visionaries are the ones that are going to be the winning side when the history books look back on this important period of time. They will be the ones to write that history, the victors that will get to show the rest of the world how it got to such a better place. Mr. Trajan might have given you some information but he would never cast aside his beliefs in favor of yours."

"It's really that hard to believe that someone could break free of your brainwashing?" Nina asked. "You are really so far gone that you can't even imagine the possibility that someone might have considered another way? The Visionaries really got into your head, didn't they? That's terrible. You need to understand that their way is not the only way."

"Maybe not," Miss Augustus said. "But it is the only way that actually matters. You will see someday... Oh wait, you won't. They will have gotten rid of you before then. Thank you for digging this up and finding the breastplate for us but hand it over now. You don't have to make this difficult."

"And if we don't?" Callie asked. "What exactly are you going to do about that? We all know that you are under strict orders not to be the ones to kill us. The Visionaries want that pleasure for themselves, right? So you are on a leash."

Miss Augustus wasn't perturbed by that. "They said that we couldn't kill you. They didn't say anything about maiming you or crippling you. They don't care if you feel an extreme amount of pain as long as they are the ones at the end that get to choose to end your miserable lives. So that's what we will do to you if you don't do as we say. We are going to make you suffer."

Mr. Aurelius chimed in behind her. "And it's going to really, really hurt."

A brawl broke out, and it was a much more even fight now that the new Triumvirate didn't have the gargantuan Mr. Trajan on their side. It was a messy, brutal fight, one that everyone was anticipating. They all wanted to put an end to the conflict once and for all. Purdue tackled Mr. Aurelius to the ground. He went down much easier than Mr. Trajan did.

Elijah stayed out of the fight, holding on to the breastplate for dear life. He did not intend to let his prize go, not after what they had gone through to get it and how much he wanted it to begin with.

Callie and Nina fought Miss Augustus but it was obvious that Callie was delivering the most blows. She was still furious that they had chosen to mimic the old Third Triumvirate. As Callie beat down Miss Augustus, it was like watching her fight herself. She kept smashing her knuckles against her opponent's mask, over and over and over, until finally, an uppercut knocked the mask clear off of her face. It clattered on the floor of the chamber.

Even without the mask, there was still a striking resemblance between the criminal and Callie. They really had chosen someone that looked so much like her. At first glance, someone could mistake them for sisters, but some of the more minor details separated them, at least in Callie's mind. The nose was more elongated, more beak-like, and her cheekbones were more prominent. Still, it was almost like looking in a mirror, though it was a warped reflection.

Purdue became momentarily distracted by the woman's face, and though it was only for a few seconds, it was long enough for Mr. Aurelius to shove him off. The masked man scurried out of the chamber, scrambling up out of the darkness of the cavern. He didn't spare any time to make his escape.

"Damn it!" Purdue yelled. "Get back here, you little bastard! I won't bite!"

Mr. Aurelius was long gone and probably had no intention of coming back. He had been worried about self-preservation and didn't seem to care at all if his accomplice made it out of that hole with him. The battle for the armor was lost anyway, so he might have seen it as a pointless fight anyway. Purdue just wished that they could have stopped him too. Then they would have had the whole set.

All that was left was Miss Augustus. She tripped over her own feet, falling backward, and tried to slink away from Callie.

"You think that you are going to make any difference?" the woman spat, her face flush with fury. "You really think that you are going to change the future!?"

"We could say the same thing to you," Callie said venomously. "You and your friends are dedicating—no, *sacrificing*. You are throwing your lives away for a group of people that do not care about you. You are doing it for a cause that does not benefit you in any real way, and that is only going to help the architects that are making sure that it will be a benefit for them. That's all you are doing. At least my Third Triumvirate was doing something that we thought would benefit everyone, and we weren't just following someone's orders. We were doing it for ourselves and for our own beliefs."

"You don't understand duty!" Miss Augustus roared. "Or loyalty! Or being a part of something so much larger than yourself! I don't care what happens to me as long as the Visionaries can continue their work in purging this world of all of the baggage that it no longer needs! If they can keep their dream alive, then I don't mind devoting my life to them. It's worth it!"

The woman was too far gone, too lost in the mentality that had been installed into her brain by the Visionaries. She couldn't see reason, and she couldn't even begin to question any of it; doubt never had a chance to even remotely develop in her mind, even when evidence was constantly being presented to her to try to get her to rethink her frame of thought. There was no way of breaking her free from the constraints that all of those disturbed philosophies had bound her with. The way she saw it, there was only one future to look forward to—the one that the Visionaries controlled.

Callie let out a sigh. "I want to help you. I really do. But you are making this so hard. Please. Let us help you get out of this, help you work through all of these delusions that they got you to believe."

"What you call a delusion, I call faith," Miss Augustus said, catching her breath. "And faith is the most important thing in the world. It helps you keep going. It keeps your morals and your beliefs anchored to something that can carry you to where you need to go. I have faith that their future is imminent and that the world will be better for it. There is nothing you can help me with because there is nothing wrong with me. You all, on the other hand, need help, or you won't even see the future that is coming."

Miss Augustus suddenly bit down on something, and there was the sound of a violent hiss. White bubbles started to pour out of her mouth as Callie pried her mouth open and tried to get that foam out of her mouth. Unfortunately, the cyanide poison worked too quickly and burned right through her, ending her life and immediately halting their further line of questioning.

Callie's eyes were wide as she tried to shake the woman into some kind of recovery, but there was nothing that could be done. It was too late the moment that she bit into that cyanide pill. She would rather end her life than betray the people that she followed so fervently. The woman called Miss Augustus would die for the Visionaries—and she did.

18

THE RETURN OF MISS CALIGULA

"That wasn't supposed to happen!"

Callie was still trying to stir the dead woman awake, but no amount of shaking or throttling was going to be able to pull her back from her demise. Purdue put a hand on her shoulder to get her to stop and help her to her feet, leaving Miss Augustus on the floor, the foam still bubbling around her mouth.

"It's too late," Purdue said. "So just leave her be, aye? It's not your fault. She wanted it to end that way. She chose to take her own life. You remember that. This is not on you."

Callie nodded but was still trembling. She hadn't expected to have to hold on to someone as they killed themselves, and it had clearly shaken her up a little bit. No one could blame her. Anyone would struggle with that kind of a shock.

"Where did the other one go?" Nina asked.

"Far away from here, probably. He cut his losses and made his big escape. I can't say I blame him. He knew that there was no way they were going to win this fight."

"Two out of three isn't bad," Elijah said. "Especially since we got this." He held up the breastplate proudly.

Purdue tried to smile back, but it still felt somewhat like a hollow victory. He could tell just from Nina's expression that she had a similar thought. They may have stopped them from getting Alexander's armor, but it didn't feel like it was over because the real threat that was pulling the Third Triumvirate's strings was still out there.

"How do you think the Visionaries are going to react to all of this?" Nina asked.

"Probably not well, aye," Purdue said. "But to hell with them. Let them cry about it."

Elijah's glee faded away as he suddenly looked deep in thought. He was staring at the floor of the chamber, directly at the mask that Miss Augustus had been wearing. "Well...what if there was a way that we could find out what the Visionaries think? What if we see firsthand what they have to say about it and maybe even learn more about them? An insider that we can plant in their ranks."

"What are you talking about?" Nina asked but followed Elijah's gaze from the mask and up to Callie.

"You have to put the mask on."

Callie looked more than a little confused. She looked annoyed. "What are you talking about?"

"Miss Augustus is dead, obviously," Elijah said. "But that doesn't mean that she can't live on in a different, yet similar, form. That is the benefit of these people wearing masks all of the time. Someone else could slip on the mask if need be and pretend to be the original wearer. Most people would be none the wiser to that kind of a trick."

Nina suddenly realized where the curator's mind was going and elaborated. "If you put on Miss Augustus's mask, you could pretend to be her and infiltrate their ranks. You could figure out where they came from and more about what they want. This could actually be a rather golden opportunity. You look enough like her to probably fool people, as long as they are not looking too closely."

"*Probably* fool people? That's reassuring." Callie crossed her arms and shook her head. "That can't be the only plan that we have. Do you have any idea how risky that would be for me to do? As much as I miss those kinds of costumes, I have no desire to put on that mask over there. That mask shouldn't even exist. It's an absolute disgrace to all of the actual hard work that myself, Mr. Nero, and Mr. Commodus put into the Third Triumvirate when we started. Having that on my face would be awful."

"Awful for you but beneficial to us," Elijah said.

"I understand your reservations, aye," Purdue said. "But right now we can't be worried about those kinds of things. We can't pass up an opportunity like this. We need something that will give us an edge over the Visionaries. We need something that they won't expect, and I don't think they are going to expect this."

Callie was hardly convinced and just seemed to be getting more and more infuriated by everyone trying to force her into agreeing with the plan. "So let me get this straight. Hopefully you will all hear how insane you sound. You want me to put on that dead woman's mask and pretend to be Miss Augustus? That way, we can use me as a mole to find out more about the Visionaries—putting my life and safety completely at risk, by the way. You think that I will somehow be able to be a perfect copy of her and not get caught? Unfortunately, I don't think I can pass off that kind of a performance. I don't know how to be her."

"You just have to do your best," Purdue said with some confidence. "The mask will be able to do the rest. The fact that you are wearing that will not only mask your identity, but it will put all of your enemies' minds at ease. They know that mask. They know who used to wear it. When they are looking at it, they aren't going to pay too much attention to the voice behind it."

"You're wrong," Callie said. "They will probably pay even more attention to my voice because they can't see my face."

"Have some confidence in yourself," Nina said. "You did all kinds of uncertain things when you were Miss Caligula. Find that part of you again, the part that isn't afraid to get her hands dirty and do whatever it takes to get what she wants."

It was nice to see Nina supporting Callie after everything that they had been through and all of the recent accusations at the start of the expedition. "Look, I don't want to force you to do this. None of us do. We have all seen how hard you have tried to move past this part of your life and put that all in the past. The problem is... that's the part of you that we need right now. We need Miss Caligula. I know it won't be easy, but I also know that you can do it if you put your mind to it."

Callie's expression softened. She seemed very touched by Nina's words of encouragement and maybe was even a little bit surprised by them too. There was a time when Callie had almost killed Nina, but now they were not only working together but helping each other be better and make the most of their talents and of their lives.

"I don't think we can do this..." Callie said. The hesitation and fear were plain as day on her face. She really did not think that something like that could work. "There are so many variables and things that can go wrong."

"And we will deal with those things when we get there," Purdue said. "We have done riskier things before."

"Maybe you have and it's easier for you to say when you are not the one that is going to be hiding behind a mask and trying to convince people that you are something that you are not. I know you all must think that this will be easy for me because, for a long time, you thought I was just pretending to want to change. But I wasn't. I was never lying about it. I'm a terrible liar. How am I supposed to pass myself off for her? These people know her. They—"

Purdue put a hand on her shoulder to try to get her to calm down before her panic completely overwhelmed her. "They are going to believe it, and if they don't, we will be right there to back you up. We haven't had this good of an opportunity to take these people by surprise before. The Visionaries keep catching us off guard, which always gives them the advantage. It's time to take that away from them and have them be caught unawares. Time to flip the script, aye?"

For the next hour or so, they constructed a plan that they hoped would be enough to help them against their foes. Its basic premise seemed simple enough, but things hardly ever went completely according to plan in those kinds of situations, not when the stakes were so high and people were aware that they had enemies.

"Here's what we do," Nina said. "You, as Miss Augustus, tell them that you found Alexander's armor and that you have killed us. You want to deliver their prize to them. We lure them to a place of our choosing where we could set a trap, capture another one of them and question them, press them for even more information."

"And we make sure that none of them have a chance to choke on a cyanide capsule this time," Purdue said. It had become a problem every time that they got the upper hand on the Visionaries and their associates. It was frustrating that their people were so devoted to the cause that they were willing to end their lives instead of spilling any secrets. First it was Eve Wayneright, and now Miss Augustus. They were lucky that Mr. Trajan hadn't done the same. "Those sick bastards just keep doing that."

"Right. Hopefully it will be one of the Visionaries themselves that comes to pick up their trophy," Elijah said. "That would make things much easier. Or, at the very least, one of their higher ranked lieutenants like Terrence was."

Callie pulled Miss Augustus's phone out of her pocket and flipped it open. It was a burner phone, meant to be discarded relatively soon after its calls couldn't be traced. She went through some of the most recent calls and saw that most of them were all to the same number, probably checking in with her bosses.

"Put it on speakerphone," Purdue whispered. "And let's have ourselves a chat."

Callie did as she was instructed and called the most frequent number, turning on the speakerphone function so everyone around them could hear the call. It rang a number of times, and with each ring, the anticipation mounted. Hopefully the person on the other end would at least pick up.

The phone kept ringing and then, with a beep, fell silent.

Everyone's anxiety grew a little bit. In order for their plan to work, they needed to at least get in touch with the people that had sent the new Third Triumvirate in the first place. They needed to lay the crumbs for them to follow before they could spring the trap, otherwise it was all for nothing.

Purdue was determined, though. "Message them. Make it clear that it's urgent but don't be too specific. Just enough to get them interested."

Callie drafted the message that she was going to send. It read: **Urgent meeting, re: the armor.**

They needed to go even further. Purdue's mind was racing. It didn't matter where they met, really, as long as they could draw one of the Visionaries out. "Tell them that you will meet them at a rendezvous point near here."

Callie tapped away on her phone. It now read: **Caligula's Vault. I will send you the location.**

"Good enough, aye," Purdue said. "Now we just have to hope that they buy into it."

For the next few minutes, they felt like fishermen sitting on a boat, waiting for one of their targets to take their bait. All they could do was hope that they would get some sort of response. Luckily, after those few nerve-racking minutes, they did.

The phone's notification pinged, and a message was on the screen.

Perfect. I am on my way.

19

CALLIE UNDERCOVER

It had been a long time since Callie had worn one of those masks, and it didn't seem to fit as well as it used to. She didn't remember it being so cumbersome and so restricting to her vision. Back when she was Miss Caligula with the Third Triumvirate, everything had seemed so clear no matter how difficult it was to see through the eye holes in her mask. Now, it just felt so much heavier, like it was trying to pull her head down off of her neck and her face clean off.

Maybe it was just the nerves. This wasn't like how it used to be. She wasn't in the midst of some operation that she fully believed in, trying to take something that she thought would end up helping in the end. No, she was in a much different circumstance, pretending to be someone else. Now there was more reason than ever not to let that mask come off and keep her identity hidden.

It was so stressful, though. She had no idea if their enemies would actually believe that she was Miss Augustus. She kind of doubted it, but she was going to try to do her best to impersonate her. She had her reservations about the whole plan, but Purdue was probably right that it was the best chance that they had to really try to figure out how to bring down the Visionaries. They needed someone on the inside, someone that could gather enough information to make a difference. It was just unfortunate that the best mole that they had was her. She was the only one that could even come close to passing for Miss Augustus, so it was up to her to be the spy.

She approached the location that they had been given, continuously adjusting the mask to make sure that it was staying on correctly. It didn't fit her as well as it probably did the person that she was pretending to be.

Somewhere nearby, Purdue and the others were keeping an eye on her, doing their best not to be seen. Potentially, they weren't the only ones watching her either. The Visionaries might already be there, surveying the scene before going down to meet her. It was going to be hard to fool them or at least keep up the act long enough to get something useful out of them.

Callie did her best to try to return to the person she had been when she was a criminal. She had to find the mastermind of the original Third Triumvirate, the woman that Miss Augustus had tried to mold herself after. She needed to dig deep into her own psyche to pull out that person that used to actually be a danger to society, that could hold her own against the worst of the worst without any fear.

She needed to find Miss Caligula.

Headlights caught her attention as a long, dark limousine approached her. It slowly rolled up, like the hidden driver was trying to be sure that they were in the right place. She really hoped that they hadn't been able to figure her out that quickly, and she tried her best to imagine how Miss Augustus usually held herself. Her posture could be the difference between life and death. When the vehicle came to a halt, it sat there for a long moment before one of its doors in the back slowly opened and remained there.

Whoever was inside the car wanted her to come in.

Callie glanced in the direction that she knew the others were watching from. They would be powerless to help her if she got into the limo, especially if it drove away. She might be going directly into her tomb if she got into the car, but there wasn't much choice. The person inside obviously wanted her to join them. Reluctantly, she approached the limousine and, after another pause, got inside.

∾

"What the hell is she doing!?" Nina asked, looking through the binoculars. "What are we supposed to do if something happens in there or if they take off with her still inside?"

"I'm sure she is aware of the risks," Purdue said through his own set of binoculars. "She's a smart girl. She knows what could happen to her, and she also knows that she is not being given a choice in the matter. They are dictating this meeting on their terms and that means deciding where the conversation is going to be taking place. It's just a power move. The Visionaries enjoy being in control of those kinds of situations. Like hiding their bloody faces behind computer screens."

That had been their way since he had first become aware of their existence. Outside of Eve Wayneright trying to recruit him, he had only met the others on a computer monitor when he first spoke to them. They were all hidden under avatars and images that did not reveal their identities. They liked the anonymity. It gave them power and strength that a lot of the rest of the world did not possess.

"And what happens if they just decide to kill her in there?" Nina asked.

Purdue repeated himself, mostly to convince himself that they were doing the right thing. "She knows the risks and, let's not forget, we also knew the risks when we came up with this idea and asked her to do this. This was our collective plan. We can't pull the plug now when we're so close. We can't get scared. We just need to have faith that she is going to succeed."

"I'm trying to believe that," Nina said, "but it's not exactly easy to do that."

"At this point, there is no point worrying about it," Elijah chimed in, sitting behind them. He didn't have binoculars but could see Callie getting into the limousine down below. "It is up to her now. Unless you plan on all three of us running down there and slashing the tires of that car, it's out of our hands. Personally, I think she can pull this off. She hasn't given me any reason to doubt that yet. She had a whole career out of being a criminal. I think she knows how to play the role."

That was a good point and was what made them think that the plan had any merit to begin with. If any of them could infiltrate the Visionaries while pretending to be someone else, it was the former Miss Caligula. She was their best chance—their only chance.

"We just have to believe in her, aye," Purdue said. "She's done well this far."

Nina wasn't so optimistic. "Yes, but anything can happen."

~

Callie climbed into the limo and was relieved that it was dimly lit inside. That darkness might help mask her ruse. She took a seat on one of the long black cushions and looked down the width of the interior to find a bald, dark-skinned man in a gray suit looking back at her. He was strikingly handsome and flashed a brilliant smile in her direction once she was seated.

The car door slammed shut behind her, and she suddenly felt very trapped; it was suffocating. The stranger's smile strangely put her at ease. He held up a wide glass of liquor and offered it to her as if she could reach him at the far end of the limousine.

"Could I get you something to drink?"

Callie did her best to mimic Miss Augustus's voice, hoping that the distance between her and the man might help negate any of the differences in their inflections. She thought about how Miss Augustus might react and decided that she wouldn't be polite. She didn't seem to have that in her, but she would be grateful toward the people to whom she seemed to have such unhinged admiration.

"I appreciate it, but I'm good." Hopefully that sounded like something Miss Augustus would say.

If the man did notice anything, he didn't let it show. His smile remained, and he seemed pleased to be there. He shrugged and downed the whole glass in one gulp, wincing at the burn that must have been going through his throat before chuckling. The drink hadn't been poisoned, at least.

The man kept his eyes on her and kept smiling as she sat there. "From the sounds of your message, you and your colleagues had finally found Alexander the Great's breastplate. Am I correct?"

"Yes," Callie said, able to speak honestly even if it wasn't the colleagues that he believed they were. "We dug it up. Had to kill those other people, though. The ones you warned us about. I know we weren't supposed to, but—"

"David Purdue, you mean?" The man's smile disappeared, and he suddenly looked gravely serious. He raised a brow and leaned forward in his seat. "You mean to tell me that you three managed to kill David Purdue? *The* David Purdue?"

"Yes," Callie said, hoping she sounded convincing. "That is exactly what I'm saying. I know it's not what you wanted, but we didn't have a choice, and Mr. Trajan decided to take things into his own hands. Things got messy and—"

"Where are the bodies?" the man interrupted, looking both intrigued and nervous. "Where can I find the corpses and confirm the kill for myself?"

"They are with the breastplate right now."

"And your colleagues are there as well?"

"Yes," Callie said. "We didn't want to leave the armor unguarded, and Mr. Aurelius thought that we could give you twice the trophy and you could look at both at the same time."

The man didn't look very pleased but he didn't quite look angry either. It was a simmering frustration that he was keeping in check, perhaps even some conflicted thoughts on how things had turned out. He shook his head, still processing the information, and pulled out his phone—but just when he was about to start dialing a number, he stopped himself and started to laugh.

His snickering made her uncomfortable like he was trying and failing to contain it. It was very off-putting to hear someone laugh while looking so concerned at the same time. He was a very hard man to read. Finally, he spoke and gave her a better understanding of what was on his mind.

"You know that David Purdue threatened us, right? He dared to actually say that he was coming after us and that he would somehow bring us all down. He thought that he could get in the way of our work, somehow keep our message from spreading. Imagine being that arrogant, to have a big enough ego to think that you can stand in the way of progress and of the inevitable future that we are trying to build. How inflated one has to be to think so highly of themselves that they alone can change fate and derail destiny. What a fool. What a stupid, stupid fool. He was amusing, though. I still remember him yelling at all of us. I was sitting there at home, watching through the camera while he pointed his finger and made his threats, pretending like he was some great threat to our cause. Some threat he turned out to be...so many empty promises of destruction. And for what?"

"He seemed like an imbecile," Callie said, with some actual honesty. Sometimes a little bit of truth made it easier to sell a lie. "But he put up more of a fight than we were expecting which is why Mr. Trajan had to go to the lengths that he did. I'm sorry. I know he wasn't ours to kill."

"Oh, please," the Visionary said, and his wide white grin was brighter than ever. "Do you really think I give a damn that you disobeyed our instructions? No. Some of the others might be upset, but I will talk them down. The most important thing is that he is finally gone. David Purdue will never be able to threaten and bother us ever again. Wayneright or Terrence should have just killed him from the start. Without him, the Order of the Black Sun will crumble."

"He wasn't the only one that we killed. There was also Dr. Nina Gould and the Black Sun's curator too. He begged for his life at the end, but we didn't listen." She hoped those sadistic embellishments were helping.

The Visionary continued to seem very impressed by everything he was hearing. "And here I thought that the three of you would end up being disappointments. There is nothing better than to be surprised. So just to be clear, the three of you not only found what we wanted but got rid of our enemies too? Now Mr. Trajan and Mr. Aurelius wait with the breastplate of Alexander and the corpses of the fools that tried to stop us?"

"Yes," Callie said. "You were right to trust us with this. Now the future can come without anything standing in the way." That also sounded like something Miss Augustus would say.

"Yes, we underestimated you, clearly. We shouldn't have. Still, I was surprised to hear from you, given the updates on your progress beforehand."

Callie didn't know what he meant. "You were?"

"Oh, yes, very." The man's wide grin remained, but there was something more demented keeping it in place and a darkening look in his eyes. "From what we heard, Mr. Trajan was beaten down and taken captive by Purdue, and you disappeared not long after that. Mr. Aurelius was quite worried about you two, but from the sounds of it, you all found each other again, reunited to salvage the mission! Truly remarkable!"

It was an error, but Callie did her best to navigate it. The best way to act was to roll with whatever came her way and adjust accordingly. It made improv so important to perform. "Yes, I didn't think you would want to hear that part of it. It was an unfortunate miscalculation that we corrected—"

"You, Mr. Trajan, and Mr. Aurelius, you mean? The three of you managed to sort it all out."

Callie suddenly had the distinct impression that the man was not nearly as convinced as she had hoped. On the contrary, it seemed as if he was the one that was giving a poor acting performance.

She mustered as firm and reassuring of a response as she could. "We did, yes."

The man burst out into a fit of hysterics, clutching his sides from laughing too hard. He kept looking back up at her and laughing again. She just sat there uncomfortably and let his fit pass. When he finally caught his breath, the man rubbed his bald head like he was trying to soothe his tickled mind.

"I'm sorry, that was just too funny. I shouldn't laugh, though. It has been a wonderful performance. As I said, I was surprised to hear from you after we heard from your colleague. Because he told us a very different story. Didn't you, Mr. Aurelius?"

The man wrapped his knuckles a couple of times on the tinted window over his shoulder, which slid open seconds later to reveal the driver of the limousine. The person behind the wheel turned and showed their masked face.

It was Mr. Aurelius—the one person that could so easily discredit her whole story.

"Mr. Aurelius, might I ask you a question?"

"Yes, sir," Mr. Aurelius said, though she could feel his hidden gaze fixed on her.

"Is this woman in this car with us the Miss Augustus that you know?"

Mr. Aurelius let out a breath that seemed to echo through the mask when he exhaled. After a long moment, he shook his head. "No. Definitely not."

Callie immediately went for the door but the locks flew down before her hands could open it. She tried to pry the lock out of the hole, but it wasn't coming out. She was stuck in the car with two enemies.

"You were so close, too," the Visionary said, leaning back casually and crossing his legs like he was having a pleasant time. "I really have to again commend that performance. There were a couple of moments there where I really might have bought into that yarn you were weaving if not for Mr. Aurelius reaching out to me first. You can imagine how that might have tainted the story a little bit. We really might have done too good of a job of making Miss Augustus take after you. You two are too similar for your own good and for my own good."

Despite all of her best efforts, their plan was doomed from the beginning. Callie could have been a perfect copy of Miss Augustus, but they still would have known the truth and suspected her from the start. There was nothing she could do—and now she was trapped.

"Take us for a drive, my friend," he said to Mr. Aurelius. "We have much to discuss with Miss Caligula."

Without any hesitation, the driver did as he was asked and the car pulled out of the lot. In moments, the limousine was on the road and driving away from the only people that might actually have been able to get Callie out of the mess that she was now in.

The man poured another glass of scotch and offered it to her once again. "I think you might really want a drink now."

Callie declined again. She didn't want anything from those people except to be released. She knew that that was not going to happen, though. She was truly stuck and at the mercy of people that would probably not hesitate to hurt her.

The man downed the liquor once again, laughing when he did before leaning forward like he was a child waiting for a book to be read to him. "Please tell me again about your valiant efforts of defeating my enemies and finding the breastplate of Alexander. What was it? You just had to kill David Purdue? He gave you no choice? But you did your duty and slayed our foes? Ah yes, what a wonderful piece of fiction."

The man was relishing how in control he was. He had absolute authority over everything within the confines of that limousine and probably in plenty of places outside of that car too. He stared at her for a long moment again before bursting into another fit of laughter.

"You can take that ridiculous mask off of your face, Miss Caligula," the man said. "Besides, it's not even yours anyway. It doesn't feel quite right, does it?"

Callie waited a moment and then ripped the mask off, tossing it onto the floor of the limousine between them. That visage stared up at the ceiling of the interior, now without any power at all. It hadn't even been able to disguise the truth as she had hoped.

"There you are. The real you. Or is the real you the criminal that you left behind? That old face you used to wear before you were domesticated by the Order of the Black Sun? Before they took out your fangs."

"The fangs are still there," Callie said. "And they're still sharp."

While she had been trying to impersonate Miss Augustus, she managed to dig up her old self—or at least some of the things she used to be able to do when she only cared about getting what she wanted. That part of her, Miss Caligula, was now at the surface, and maybe it would be enough to help her escape that limo.

"I'm sure," the man snickered. "But I doubt that they are sharp enough. Let me tell you a little bit about myself, Miss Caligula."

The fact that the mysterious man was going to reveal anything told her that he probably did not intend for her to leave that vehicle alive. He wouldn't be sharing anything with her otherwise, especially with how much the Visionaries loved remaining hidden and unknowable.

She didn't have any choice but to listen to him, though.

"My name is Damon Meyer, and as I am sure you have surmised, I am one of the Visionaries that you and your friends decided to antagonize. That you and your friends decided to piss off. But I am not like Eve

Wayneright. I am not someone that you can just back into a corner. I am the Visionary with the grandest hopes and the wildest dreams, and I am the one with the most ambition, the most *vision*. The one that is most determined to get the tomorrow that I want and to make sure that it happens the way that it should. You all made a very big mistake trying to take that away from me."

The man was still smiling and still calm, but she could feel anger in his voice, pouring out and filling the car with malice and disdain. She could see just by the way he looked at her that he looked down at her, that he saw her as nothing more than an insignificant little creature that was only there to irritate him—or as something that he could just play with while he was bored and in need of entertainment.

"When your friend David Purdue decided that he was going to declare war on us and make all of his big statements about destroying us, he should have realized that we were not just going to stand for that. If he wanted to turn it into a battle, then he should have known that those kinds of things always have casualties. Maybe he did. Maybe he thought that we would both suffer losses and that those losses might be worth it. Maybe he thought that you were expendable to him. I don't claim to know how that moron thinks, but all I can tell you is that he made a poor choice that is going to cost him. We aren't going to boast about tearing down his work or destroying his life. We are just going to do it. That's how things like this should be handled. You don't have to announce it. You can keep your mouth shut and just get it done."

Callie felt so unsafe. She wanted nothing more than to break free of that car and get as far away from this Damon Meyer as possible. He seemed like the kind of man that was not afraid to take action to send a message.

"He was watching, wasn't he? David Purdue. He saw you get into the vehicle, no?"

She didn't answer. She didn't owe him anything, especially not information.

"That's alright," Damon snickered. "You wanted to find out more information about the Visionaries? Well, here you are. I'm willing to help you if you help me. So, no tall tale this time... Where is the breastplate of Alexander?"

20

PURSUIT

Purdue needed that limousine to stop, but those tires kept turning as it zoomed away from the lot and disappeared around the bend. There was no chance of intercepting it or knocking it off the road. All he could do was stand there like a fool while Callie was taken away to parts unknown. He hoped that it meant that she had convinced them well enough with that mask, but the suddenness of the departure made him think otherwise. That felt calculated, like they knew that others were close by or that they didn't want to give her a chance to leave the car.

"How do you think it went?" Elijah asked, looking in the direction that the limo had sped off to. "Do you think they bought it?"

Purdue went with his gut instinct. "No. I don't think they did."

Suddenly, his phone buzzed in his pocket. He pulled it out but didn't recognize the name at all. Usually, he would ignore those calls, but something told him that it would be a good idea to answer it.

"Oi?"

"David Purdue. The one that decided to take on the future."

Purdue scoffed, "Aye, that's me. And who am I speaking to?"

"Don't you remember me?" the voice snickered. "Of course you don't. I didn't speak, and you didn't get a look at my face. I was one of those people that you decided to threaten and scream at on Eve Wayneright's computer. Do you remember? All of those horrible things you said to us...so scary."

Purdue knew exactly who he was speaking to, but this time the person was speaking back. "You are one of the Visionaries, aye?"

"That's right. One that is tired of your continued existence."

"Sorry that I keep breathing air," Purdue said. "I can't really help that, though...human nature and all of that. I'm sure that you understand."

"You sound nervous, Mr. Purdue," the man said. "Don't tell me that you're frightened by us now? What happened to all of the bravery and all of the stupidity of actually saying that you were going to come find us and get rid of us? Where did that David Purdue go?"

"Listen, I'm typically a man of my word, and I have every intention of following through on everything that I said to you all then. I am going to track you down, kick your ass, and stop you from destroying the history of this world."

"You are, huh? You made those big claims, but then you didn't seem to follow through. I kept waiting for a knock on my door or a phone call...something that showed that you were at least closing in. But you never did."

The man on the other end of the phone call just started laughing hysterically before composing himself. "Let's get down to business, shall we? The Visionaries and the Order of the Black Sun keep hurting one another. Back and forth, and back and forth. It will go on forever if we're not careful. So let's have a moment of good faith and restore some of the balance that has been lost here."

"Meaning what?"

"I am suggesting a trade, Mr. Purdue. A simple exchange. You hand over Alexander's breastplate and I give you back the imposter that you tried to trick us with. Oh, and if you would be so kind as to return Mr. Trajan to us as well. That seems like a fair trade, doesn't it? Surely, Miss Caligula's life is worth the armor and Mr. Trajan? That is more than reasonable, I must say."

Purdue put his hand over the phone and swore under his breath. The Visionaries knew what his weaknesses were and what to exploit. They knew perfectly well that he wasn't just going to give up on one of his allies. That was the kind of thing that separated him from people like them. They didn't want Mr. Trajan to come back because they were worried for his safety. They wanted him back because it was another piece that they could use to get the upper hand on the Order of the Black Sun.

"I would like an answer, Purdue. You either agree to the terms and we make the exchange, or I kill your friend right here and now. It really wouldn't take much, and I would be doing this world a favor. There would be one less criminal to relapse and fall back into her old ways. She can pretend that she has changed all she wants, but I'm sure you all still know the truth. There is no redemption for someone like her. Maybe I should kill her right now because you obviously don't think she's worth the—"

"I'll do it," Purdue said quickly. "I will, aye. There's no need to do anything except make the bloody trade."

"Look at that. The great David Purdue can be reasoned with...if enough pressure is applied, of course."

21

THE EXCHANGE

Purdue was just relieved that they hadn't left Mr. Trajan back in Alexandria. Instead, they had kept him tied up in one of the closets inside the private jet. That seemed like a comfortable place for him to fly.

The meeting place for the exchange was not far from Caligula's secret vault. Elijah stood beside Purdue, still clutching that piece of armor like he would never let go— but now he had to. He looked absolutely depressed by how the situation had turned out.

When the limousine pulled up, Damon Meyer stepped out of the vehicle and then heaved something out from the back of the car. It was Callie, looking worse for wear. Her mouth was covered by a rope tied around her skull, shoved between her teeth. Her eyes were wide, but it also looked like she was struggling to keep them open.

She looked so exhausted. They must have put her through a lot during her captivity.

Damon stood beside Callie, keeping his hand grasped around her arm to keep her from running away. She looked like she was in pain and about to topple over. The Visionary had clearly put her through an ordeal.

Purdue pointed to the armor at his feet and the hulking figure beside him. "I brought what you asked for, so stick to your end of the deal, aye? I give you your big bastard back along with the breastplate, and you let her go."

"Of course," Damon said. "As agreed upon. Let Mr. Trajan go. Mr. Trajan, you will come over here. Then place the armor over here. After that, I will release Miss Caligula and we can all go about our business with the transaction complete."

It was annoying that he was the one dictating the specific terms of how things were going to be handled, but he really was in the greatest position of power among all of them. If they made one wrong move, Callie could be seriously harmed, and none of them wanted that. The whole point of the exchange was to rescue her, so doing anything that would put her in harm's way was the wrong choice.

Purdue let Mr. Trajan walk forward and go back to his accomplices. The man lumbered slowly, but the smile on his face was so frustrating to see. He was obviously loving being able to just walk free from his captors. It made Purdue sick to see that he was just going to get away after all of the trouble they had gone through with him. The behemoth took a spot beside Damon Meyer and Mr. Aurelius. He looked back and winked at Purdue, Nina, and Elijah.

Next, Elijah picked up the breastplate of Alexander and lugged it toward their enemies. He was absolutely livid to be giving them the relic. There was nothing that he hated more than those priceless artifacts ending up in the wrong hands. Willingly allowing that to happen—even if he was being forced to—was a betrayal of everything that he believed in. Still, he knew that a life was on the line and placed the breastplate a few feet away from their foes. Once it was on the ground, he glared at them and just shook his head before walking back.

Purdue stepped forward now, ready to finalize the exchange. "Let Callie go. Right now."

Damon Meyer grinned. "Of course. As we discussed."

The man released his grip on Callie's arm and shoved her forward. She nearly tripped as she stumbled over toward them. They could hear that she was trying to shout something, but it was muffled by the rope in her mouth. They couldn't understand what she was saying, even as she drew closer. Purdue hurried over to intercept her, to at least get her out of the restraints.

Behind her, Damon and Mr. Aurelius started splashing what looked like gasoline onto the breastplate of Alexander, and after a few dumps of the black liquid, Damon ignited a lighter and tossed it onto the soaked artifact. It went up flames immediately, engulfing the famous armor.

Elijah nearly charged them. "No! No! No! What the hell are you doing!?"

"Are you really so startled by this?" Damon snickered. "What did you think was going to happen? Did you think that we were just going to hold on to it for safekeeping? We have a job to do, and that involves destroying that ridiculous vest."

Purdue couldn't worry too much about the breastplate. It was just the unfortunate inevitability considering who they were up against. He was much more concerned with Callie, who seemed so weak when he reached her and started cutting her loose. It took a minute for him to finally get that rope out of her mouth and off of her head. When he did, he saw blood coming out over her lips and realized that she looked like she was about to faint.

"Callie...oi, you're alright. We're here now. You are okay..."

She definitely didn't look okay, and when he held her hips to keep her steady, he felt something warm and wet on his palm. He looked at his hand and found that it was stained with blood that was seeping through her shirt.

"I'm...I'm sorry, Purdue...he stabbed me before...before we got here."

Callie would have collapsed to the ground if Purdue wasn't there to keep her steady. The realization that she was bleeding out was making it hard for him to stay calm. It was taking all of his willpower to keep it together. He craned his head to address Nina. "Hey! I need help over here!"

"What is it!?" Nina rushed over and immediately saw the source of the panic. Her expression grew grave at the sight of that blood and the condition that Callie was in. "Oh my god."

Purdue felt utter contempt come over him and looked past Callie to her captor. "What the hell is this? The deal was that you let her go!"

"I did, didn't I?" Damon shrugged. "Our deal said nothing about what kind of condition she had to be in when she was returned to you. That is an unfortunate oversight on your part but it does not break the arrangement we made."

Between the burning breastplate and the wounded friend, Elijah started to rush at them, but Damon pulled out a pistol and smirked when Elijah's charge came to a halt. "I wouldn't. The rest of you can keep your lives today for however much more of a future you have left. You should be happy about that and just leave it at that. And you may want to get your friend to the nearest medical facility. She might need a stitch or two."

"You son of a bitch!" Purdue cried as Callie fell to the ground, not able to stand anymore. The blood loss was really starting to take its toll. Her skin was turning white and her eyes were struggling to stay open. "Why the hell would you do this!?"

Damon Meyer seemed perfectly content with his decision to wound her. "She was no different than all of the other things of the past that are no longer needed, and we get rid of things like that. She had no place in the world that we are making."

Purdue was ready to rip the man to pieces. The Visionaries continued to show how ruthless they were and how little they actually cared about other human beings. They were disgusting monsters that had no right trying to dictate to other people, let alone to try to change the whole world. Human society could be ugly enough without people like them calling all of the shots.

Nina was trying her best to keep Callie calm. "It's okay, Callie. You're going to be alright. It's not that bad. It's not that bad."

"You're lying..." Callie said with a weak smile, trembling. "I can tell."

Callie was growing weaker by the second, her eyes fluttering with the last vestiges of life that she had left. She looked from Nina to Purdue, and tears started to well in her eyes. "I'm sorry...I'm so sorry..."

"For what?" Nina asked, running a hand through the young woman's hair. "You didn't do anything wrong."

Callie choked out some blood. Every breath was becoming more and more of a struggle. "I'm sorry that I ever...I'm sorry that I ever gave you guys any reason to doubt me...I really...I really wanted to be a part of the group. I know it was hard...it was hard for me too...to make up for everything that I did to you...and I'm sorry for all of it..."

"All of that is in the past," Nina said. "It's gone. It's forgotten. Don't worry about that now, okay? We are the ones that should apologize for taking so long to give you a chance. Sam knew right away, but the rest of us were so thickheaded. I'm the one that's sorry, Callie. You're not the person that I fought in the coliseum. You changed. You changed for the better."

Callie managed a smile. "My name isn't Callie..."

Obviously not. They all figured it was just an alias and a play off of her Miss Caligula moniker, but Purdue was surprised to hear her open up about it, considering that she never had before.

"My real name is Giana. That's who I am without any... without any masks..."

With that, Callie's eyes stopped blinking and remained fixated on Nina above her. The rest of her body grew still, and the young woman died in the arms of the people that used to be her enemies.

Purdue had never seen Nina look so guilt-ridden before. She hugged the young woman tightly, an embrace that was so regretful, like she was trying to make up for so much time wasted.

The former Miss Caligula was dead.

22

ARMOR

It was hard to believe that Callie was gone, killed just when she was supposed to be freed. After everything they had given up to get her back... The trick was so callous and horrible.

Purdue stood up and pointed at Damon and his cronies. "You think this is just going to end like this? I'm not going to stand for it. You bastards are going to burn for what you have done today. I promise you. You are going to fucking burn."

"Ah yes, more threats from David Purdue. Don't you have any other tricks? All of your empty promises and scary warnings have amounted to...this. Well done. You should never have made such bold claims that you could never actually follow through on."

"I will follow through on them," Purdue growled. "You can guarantee that, you piece of shit."

"Have you learned nothing from all of this? When you declared war on the Visionaries, David Purdue, you declared war on the future itself. How could you possibly hope to win against that? The tides of change stop for no one. They can only be redirected, and that is what we are doing. You just put yourself in the tidal wave's path. And that is not a good place to be. You won't survive. If you want you and your friends and that secret society that you tried so hard to refurbish...if you want that all to survive...then you will stop your ridiculous resistance. You will stand aside and allow the future to unfold. This is your last warning. There won't be another chance. I suggest you accept it and go home."

With that, Damon Meyer turned around and walked away as if nothing had happened. He left them with the ruined breastplate and Callie's corpse. All they had managed to get from this expedition was death and destruction.

Purdue was not satisfied. He wasn't ready to let these Visionaries continue to run rampant and hurt them. He was tired of them and wanted them to be ended. He wanted to bury them and forget about them just like he had done to his previous enemies. He didn't accept the future that they had in mind.

Purdue grabbed hold of the scorched armor and was surprised that it wasn't hot to the touch. The fire was even dissipating and the metal of the breastplate didn't look like it had even been badly damaged despite being engulfed in flames. Maybe it was thanks to whatever properties helped it protect its wearer. Whatever the case, Purdue was pleased and pulled it over his head, strapping it onto his torso.

"What the hell are you doing, Purdue?" Elijah asked, but he was looking at the armor with a befuddled expression. "The breastplate—"

"I think it's fine," Purdue said. "Luckily." He glanced back at Callie's body on the ground and Nina tending to it. "She's not, though, and I'm not letting that son of a bitch get away with it. The Visionaries think that they've won again, but I'm not done. Not yet."

Elijah looked concerned but understanding. "Alright. Just bring that breastplate back in one piece."

"I don't think you have to worry about that," Purdue said. "It seems to do a pretty good job of protecting itself."

With that, Purdue sprinted in the direction that the Visionary and his cronies had walked in. They weren't going to escape. They were probably celebrating, but he was going to make sure that their victory was very short-lived. He was being fueled by so much pent-up frustration and newfound anger after this exchange. They weren't going to get away with more of their madness.

It didn't take long for Purdue to catch up to them at the pace that he was going, especially when they were so casually strolling away from such a terrible situation. They were arrogant, and he was going to make them regret ever thinking that they won.

Purdue called out to them when he got close, "Where do you think you're going, you bastards!?"

Damon Meyer turned around and the two men flanking him did the same. The Visionary looked more amused than surprised, while Mr. Trajan and Mr. Aurelius were hard to read, given the masks that were back on their faces.

Purdue stopped when he got within about fifteen feet of them, letting them realize that the fight was not over yet. They didn't get to dictate the meeting or decide when it ended, especially when they had sabotaged the agreed-upon exchange.

"We had an agreement," Purdue said. "I don't know about you, but I really don't like when people break those kinds of deals. We stuck to our end, and then you went and had to do that to Callie."

"Miss Caligula deserved exactly what she got," Damon said. "And she has you and your ego to thank for that. You were the one that started all of this. We wanted to welcome you into our ranks and you decided to get in the way of our mission instead. You are the reason that girl is dead, not me. I just finished what you started."

"Go to hell," Purdue said. "I made you all a promise that I was going to bring you down. And like I said, I'm a man of my word."

"How many times are we going to have to show you that you don't stand a chance against us?" Damon growled. His gaze shifted to Purdue's chest. "I'm surprised that the breastplate isn't roasted by now. I guess it's not so easy to destroy something like that. We will just have to figure that out. Thank you for bringing it back to us and bringing that to our attention. Mr. Trajan, please be so kind and remove that breastplate from Mr. Purdue's chest."

The tall, lumbering monster of a man stepped forward. "With pleasure."

After the torture that they had put him through, the giant thief was probably happy to have a chance to get some retribution. Still, he wasn't in his best shape after what his body had been put through. In most cases, he would have crushed Purdue, but now the odds might have been evened out a little bit.

Mr. Trajan charged like a bull and went to tackle Purdue to the ground. When his arms wrapped around Purdue's chest, though, a strange feeling came over Purdue, and he suddenly felt like he was a boulder that could not be moved. His body felt so strong, and the member of the Third Triumvirate could not bring him down. A power radiated from the breastplate and enveloped its wearer, giving him the strength to keep him safe from the attack.

The legends about that breastplate were clearly true.

Purdue felt like he could conquer the world while wearing it.

Mr. Trajan let out a grunt of confusion. It was probably the first time that he hadn't been able to use his enormous size to take someone down. He kept pushing, trying to wrangle his enemy, but Purdue wouldn't budge.

With the power protecting him, Purdue decided to just focus on his attack and started punching away at the man's head. His fists crashed against the side of his skull, avoiding the mask on his face, but then he threw a punch that cracked that mask and sent Mr. Trajan onto his stomach, unconscious. Purdue felt untouchable with that power radiating off of him. He didn't have to worry about defending himself while that breastplate was on him.

Damon Meyer watched the whole thing with some fascination. "You see now why we have to destroy things like that armor, David Purdue? We need to because there are old magics that should not exist, that are dangerous to the balance of the world. That thing on your chest is something that does not belong in the modern world, something that we can never fully understand—and that's dangerous."

"I don't know," Purdue said. "I think the secrets from the past can sometimes spice things up nowadays, aye? It's just people like you that are afraid of it because you don't know how to control it. And with you, it's all about control, isn't it? That's all you really care about."

"Enough of this. The others will just have to accept that I was the one that got rid of you for good."

Damon Meyer pulled a pistol out from his jacket and aimed it at Purdue's face. He smiled behind the barrel of that gun as he squeezed the trigger, and a shot rang out.

Purdue flinched as the bullet flew straight toward his head. He didn't have time to try to avoid it or block it with something. It would have smashed straight through his cranium if not for the power coming off of the armor he wore. It created something of an invisible barrier, enshrouding him completely in its protections. The bullet found itself caught in that power, crashing into that barrier, and was deflected back in the direction that it came from.

The bullet flew back toward the one that fired it. Damon Meyer looked horrified as the bullet whizzed past him, grazing the side of his face and going right across his eye socket. He let out a cry of pain as blood poured from his eye. He stumbled backward, shrieking, the gun falling to the ground. His own weapon had backfired on him, thanks to the power of Alexander's armor. His attack was useless against that kind of power, and he had done nothing but hurt himself.

The Visionary writhed on the ground as Mr. Aurelius tried to help him, but Damon was inconsolable. He held his hand over his left eye as blood seeped through his fingers. That stray bullet had done some real damage to him, maybe even blinding that eye. He looked up, and his one visible eye was wide with rage when he leered at Purdue.

"Kill him!" Damon roared. "Kill him right now!"

Mr. Aurelius, just trying to do his best to follow the command, picked up the pistol and started firing wildly at Purdue. He should have known better after seeing what happened to his superior. The five shots that he unleashed all reflected back at him, and the man was riddled with his own bullets, immediately falling onto his back. He lay there in a heap as he bled out from the wounds.

The only two people that were still conscious or alive were Purdue and Damon Meyer. The breastplate had turned the tables of the battle so quickly. The smugness that Damon had the entire time they had been speaking was gone. He was still groaning and seething on the ground, his hand pressed over his eye tightly, trying to stop the bleeding.

"I will kill you for this, you little shit. I will kill you for this."

"So now you're the one making threats that you can't actually follow through on," Purdue said, relishing seeing one of the Visionaries like that. "As long as I have this on, you can't touch me. Look at what just happened."

Purdue walked over and crouched down in front of his wounded enemy. As risky as it was to be that close, he wanted to show that there was nothing that Damon could do to him, no matter how much he wanted to hurt him.

"You've lost, Damon," Purdue said. "We got the breastplate and we are going to keep it safe. And clearly, it's going to keep us safe as well, aye? You and your friends need to stop this. History is not something that needs to be destroyed. It is something that should be learned from. The sooner you all get that, the sooner we can stop all of this senseless violence. You wouldn't have shot your own eye out."

Damon wasn't hearing any of it. He glared up with his good eye and spat on Purdue. The glob of phlegm was apparently not a big enough threat for the breastplate to stop. The spit landed on the old metal and slowly slid off of it. Purdue looked down at that small, pathetic sign of defiance and shook his head.

"I told you all that I was coming for you, and I am," Purdue said. "But I'm not you. I could kill you right now. I could take out another one of you, but I'm not the same as you all. I respect what came before and hope that it can be used to help change the future. I want you to learn from this, you stupid bastard. I want you to see how futile all of your efforts are. You did all of this to try to hurt us. And while you did, we still won in the end. So let's stop this. Go back to the other Visionaries and tell them what happened. Maybe they'll see what happened to you and finally come to their senses. The future is coming either way, but it doesn't need to be controlled."

Damon shook his head, his hand growing quite red with the blood coming out of his eye. He got to his feet and looked down at Purdue with his unharmed eye. "This doesn't change anything, Purdue. You won one battle in a war that you started. That's all. All this tells me is that we need to stop treating this as a game and end this as soon as possible. You are going to die. You won't be in the future that we have so carefully been crafting."

"I guess we'll just have to see," Purdue said. "Until tomorrow, then."

Damon looked a little surprised that Purdue was actually letting him go. Maybe it would have been smarter to kill him right then and there. He was obviously going to be an issue in the future that he kept clamoring about. Still, Purdue didn't need more people dying. More than enough blood had been spilled, and taking the Visionary's eye seemed like a good enough way to end this particular skirmish.

Damon Meyer slowly walked away, still holding his injured eye. Purdue watched him disappear into his limousine, having to drive himself now.

23

EULOGY FOR THE REDEEMED

"I shouldn't have been so hard on her when she first joined," Nina said.

"She understood why you were," Purdue said. "She knew that she had a lot of mistakes that she had to make up for. She knew it wasn't easy for us to forgive her for the things that she had already done to us."

"That doesn't make it any better," Nina said. "Our version of the Order of the Black Sun is supposed to be about second chances, about giving the Black Sun a better name than it used to have. We preached about that while I made her feel like she was not capable of changing, that she was always going to be bad. I shouldn't have said all of those things to her, treated her that way."

"It's too late for apologies and regrets," Elijah said bluntly, looking over the breastplate of Alexander instead of focusing at all on the fresh corpse on the ground. "She probably can't hear you, Nina."

"Do you have to be so insensitive?"

"It's just the truth," Elijah said. "Sometimes the truth hurts."

"Just have a little bit of tact, Elijah," Purdue said, but he knew that that was a lot to ask from the curator. His social cues were not always the best.

Elijah seemed to completely ignore the conversation, still fixated on the breastplate he was examining. He obviously had no interest in grieving for Callie. He barely seemed to even notice that she was gone. His obsession with inanimate objects over living beings sometimes made Purdue very uncomfortable, but it was what made the curator so good at his job too. That passion was so acutely directed—it just came at the cost of a lot of other things.

"Callie knew that we were her friends in the end," Purdue said. "She would not have told us her real name otherwise."

He firmly believed that. As tumultuous as the beginning of their association was, the former Miss Caligula had earned their respect and trust. He knew that Callie believed that in the end, even after so much suspicion and paranoia.

"That mask, her past in the Third Triumvirate, did not define her. She was not our enemy in the end. She was someone that helped us. She was our friend."

～

When they returned to the compound, Sam Cleave didn't take the news about Callie's death well. He immediately fell back into the chair he had risen from and buried his head in his hands. It was rare to see him get so upset, especially about another member of the Order of the Black Sun. It had taken him a long time to even accept that they needed other people helping them or that the people that they surrounded themselves with in the secret society could actually be helpful too.

Callie was different, though.

When Sam had been a prisoner and tortured by Julian Corvus, he was saved by Callie when she decided to turn on Julian. She had been his salvation, the saving grace that pulled him from all of that pain, torment, and despair. She had given him a chance at freedom and a chance to heal, and all that she asked in return was that he help her find some peace too.

Sam was the whole reason—maybe the only reason—that Callie had even been inducted into the Order of the Black Sun. The others would probably never have let her join but he was adamant that he trusted her, that she had saved his life, and that she deserved a place among them. It was a decision that a lot of people doubted; even Purdue and Nina, his closest allies, thought that Sam might be making some kind of horrible mistake. But in the end, as history had shown, he was proven to be right about her.

"How did she die?" Sam asked, his face still shrouded by his hands. He sounded forlorn, his lips quivering as he spoke.

Purdue was honest and told him all about the events that had transpired with the Visionaries, the fake Third Triumvirate, and Damon Meyer. As he recalled everything that they had been through in recent days, he could feel the anger emanating from his friend.

"I should have been there," Sam said. "You should have taken me with you."

"At least one of us needed to stay behind and keep running things here," Nina said.

"Then it shouldn't have been me," Sam said bitterly. "I could have...I could have done something."

"I know this isn't easy for you to hear, but we all did our best to protect Callie," Purdue said. "Really. I don't know if you would have been able to make a difference. It seemed like we were going to be able to get her back safe and sound, but that bastard tricked us."

"Is he dead?"

"What?" Purdue asked, confused by the sudden question.

"That prick that stabbed her. The Visionary guy. Is he dead?"

Purdue breathed in to try to speak as softly as possible. Sam was already upset and really didn't want to make him feel worse. Still, the truth was the truth. "No. He's still alive. He lost an eye, but...I spared his life."

Sam let out a low groan as he sunk further into his own hands and into his own grief. They could hear him let out some tears as he trembled at the table. Finally, he spoke, and his voice was cold and full of rage.

"Then I really should have been there."

Nina motioned for Purdue to follow her out of the room. They needed to give Sam some time with his grief. He had just lost one of his friends, someone that had saved his life before. More than anything, he probably wished that he could have returned the favor. Now he would never get the chance.

Once the two of them were alone, Nina faced him and crossed her arms.

"He has a point, Purdue. Why didn't you kill Damon Meyer?"

"It didn't feel right," Purdue said. "Mercy and compassion is the only thing that separates us from them."

"How many times are we going to do things like that that are inevitably going to come back and hurt us more?" Nina asked, exasperated. "How many times did we make that same mistake before against other people that caused us so much pain? We did the same thing with Julian Corvus!"

"To be fair, Julian was downright impossible to kill. We had no choice but to spare his life because we couldn't exactly take it."

"We need to stop doing this!" Nina yelled. "We can't keep trying to take the higher road! The higher road leads to awful things! We can't keep making that same mistake! We need to make whatever choice is going to benefit us and keep us safe in the end! That is what is important! Keeping our people—keeping the Order of the Black Sun—safe! That breastplate is great...but we can't all wear it."

Her words stung a lot, especially considering what happened to Callie. Usually, being compassionate and merciful felt like the right thing to do, but suddenly Purdue felt very stupid. Maybe he should have just put Damon out of his misery and taken his life along with his eye. That would have helped ensure the safety that she was talking about.

"It's not just about us anymore, Purdue. We have brought all of these people into the fold. When we reestablished the Order of the Black Sun, we took on the responsibility of having these people at our side but also doing whatever we could to keep them safe. We can't lose sight of that. It's not just us that are in danger when we do things like make new enemies."

There it was. She was still upset with him for his initial introduction to the Visionaries. "You still don't think I should have threatened them."

Nina let out a telling sigh but tried to reel in any resentment that she had. "Look, all I am saying is that maybe that was not the best way to handle it. We had just beaten Julian. We didn't need to make enemies of strangers that..."

Purdue couldn't believe what he was hearing. He knew that he sometimes made mistakes and that he sometimes did things that Nina didn't agree with, but he couldn't believe just how she was condemning him for going after the Visionaries. He wished that he could control the anger that was bubbling in him, but he couldn't. He let it out and couldn't stop whatever words were going to come out of his mouth.

"They are going to burn every bit of history to the ground, Nina! You of all people should understand why we can't just let that happen! Whether I threatened them or not, they were still going to go through with their plans! At least with what I did, they knew that they weren't just going to get away with it. I am trying to protect the things that we love! Have I done it perfectly? No! But I had to try!"

There was a long silence between them that seemed to sap away all of the yelling and simmering resentments. A quiet understanding started to encapsulate them as they both reconsidered the things that they said.

"We can't fall apart..." Purdue muttered. "We all have to stand together. If we don't, these sick bastards are going to ruin everything. I don't want that. Do you?"

"Of course I don't," Nina said. She seemed to hear him, maybe even understand the points that he was making. "You know that. I just wish there had been another way."

"Me too," Purdue said honestly. "Me too."

24

THE CURATOR'S COMPASSION

Purdue needed to get away from Nina and Sam for a little bit. The two of them kept looking at him with so much disappointment and even some bitterness. It was clear that they at least partially blamed him for what happened, even if they were trying to be understanding. He hated letting them down. It was the worst feeling in the world.

The Order of the Black Sun compound was full of historians, archaeologists, and other people that were so passionate about finding lost artifacts. It was brimming with optimism and anticipation, along with people scrambling to go on their expeditions to seek out some of the world's wonders. Usually, it was an inspiring place to be, surrounded by so many like-minded individuals. But Purdue wasn't in the mood to be around all of that commotion. He needed to find someplace where he could rest his thoughts.

There was only one place in the Order of the Black Sun headquarters that was guaranteed to be quiet: the vault room.

The large metal doors opened, and Purdue quietly stepped inside the place. As always, there were some relics in glass cases and bookshelves of ancient scrolls as he walked through the chamber. And, like there usually was, there was only one other person occupying the room.

Elijah Dane hardly ever noticed when people came into the vault room. He was usually too busy at his workstation examining whatever piece of history had most recently been brought to him. This time was no different as he paid no mind to Purdue coming inside.

It wasn't until Purdue spoke that he even realized he was there. "Do you mind if I just hang out in here for a little bit? I just have to clear my mind, aye?"

"Do whatever you want, oh fearless leader," Elijah said, still not looking up at him.

The breastplate of Alexander the Great was on his table, and he was looking over it with all kinds of magnifying devices. He was enraptured by his work and evidently didn't care why Purdue was there as long as he didn't cause too much of a disruption.

Purdue took a seat at one of the stools and stared up at the ceiling. It was exactly what he needed, a quiet room where no one was talking about what came next or why something hadn't happened differently before. The vault room was a place where the past was respected, the future was so beautifully unknown, and the present seemed to be at a standstill. It was wonderful, and he had never really noticed how serene it was before.

The two men just sat in silence, thinking about completely different things. They were alone in their minds, but at least their physical presences weren't completely alone. Finally, after a few minutes, Elijah looked over at him from behind his glasses.

"You know, most people only come to visit me when they have something for me. You have already brought me this breastplate...and the only other time someone comes to see me is if they want to drag me out onto some field operation. You've already done that too. So I have to ask, Purdue, what are you doing in the vault? Is there an old relic that you wanted to look at or something instead of just sitting there like some kind of mannequin?"

"No," Purdue said. "I just needed some peace and quiet. That's all."

"This is indeed the right place for that, I'll admit. But what brought on this need for solitude? You are usually too much of a social butterfly for that."

"What happened out there has been eating away at me a little bit, especially with how some of the others are taking it. Callie's death hit harder than I ever expected it would. I guess you sometimes don't realize how big of an impact someone had until they are gone."

"Oh, I understand that," Elijah said and pointed down to the deep vault where the most valuable of artifacts were stored and protected. "Most of those things didn't have nearly as much value until their owners were long dead. That is absolutely a sign that something really did have a lasting impact."

Purdue understood what he meant. It was the things that people left behind that mattered, including the feelings that they brought on when they were gone.

"But if it makes you feel any better, objectively speaking, I don't think that you were responsible for what happened to Callie. You should not blame yourself for something that you could not control. Her death was brought about by a series of events and a series of choices. It is not all on you. All of history is dictated by millions upon millions of small moments that lead to an inevitable point. That is all this was. To think that you had any real effect on that is nothing more than your admittedly large ego."

In his own way, the curator was actually comforting him. It was strange to be feeling better during a conversation with Elijah Dane. He usually had a way of making you feel like a fool or at least making you feel like you were somehow insignificant in the large scheme of the world and of history. He still was doing that, but it was in a helpful way.

"Take this breastplate, for instance. Think of the journey that it has been through, but it had no control over any of those events. It was forged and supposedly blessed by the

Greek gods, worn by Alexander the Great himself through his conquests, and then taken by one of the most notorious and vile emperors that ever befell the Roman Empire. Think about that. All of those choices and all of those things just happened to collide until, eventually, it now ended up in our hands. No one is solely to blame for any of that happening. It is all just events that lead into one another through time, one after the other. That is the way this universe works. No one is to blame."

Purdue understood what he was saying. It wasn't worth beating yourself up over guilt when time kept moving forward and things kept on happening that would lead to other things happening. It was an inevitable, unstoppable push forward that people could not control. It was not worth bearing the blame for something that might have been outside of his control, just like with Callie.

"These Visionaries, however..." The curator finally pulled his undivided attention away from the armor and locked eyes with Purdue. He pushed up his glasses so that he could see him more clearly. "What are we going to do about them?"

Purdue threw up his arms in defeat and shrugged. "I'm at a loss when it comes to that. Just when I think that I have done the right thing, someone tells me that I completely messed it up. So I'm probably the wrong person to ask about that. I don't have a good answer to that question."

"Perhaps I can provide my own insight then," Elijah said. "Speaking as someone that does not usually go on these expeditions but that you have somehow gotten to go on multiple field assignments...these people are the most dangerous individuals that we have ever come up against. I hated Julian Corvus. He made my life a living hell, but I would gladly take a confrontation with that psychopath over what these people are. Their ambitions are warped, but they don't seem to see that. The worst part is...those dreams of theirs are not entirely impossible."

"What do you mean?"

"Think about this room. Think about the deep vault. They are filled with all of the relics that we have all spent our time and energy collecting. There is a finite number of them, and they are tangible things. It is not out of the question that they could be destroyed or ruined forever. A person is capable of doing that. Except for maybe this breastplate and the protections on it, which seem to be quite powerful. Those others, though...most of those could be destroyed by these Visionaries."

"They can destroy the artifacts and the antiques, but they can't get rid of history."

"Of course they can," Elijah said, snapping a finger at him like he was trying to get Purdue to see sense. "These Visionaries are obviously in positions of power and probably doing everything they can to rise even higher in the world. History is not some concrete concept. It is something that can be twisted, that can be changed, and that can be disposed of. If you destroy parts of it, the things that we can touch and know are real...and then you alter the intangible parts of it, rewrite the histories of the world that can be found in books or on the internet…then you can shatter history as we know it. All we will have is memory, but even memory can be taken away, and the parts that don't still may fade over time without evidence or reminders of the truth. These people want to destroy the past, and they very well could."

Purdue hadn't thought about the Visionaries in such grand terms before, but the curator was making a lot of sense. History was dictated by the victors, that was a common expression, and there was some truth to that. If the Visionaries managed to put themselves on top of the world, then they would be the ones that dictated how the past was perceived, contort it into something false and let the truth be forgotten.

"Now are you starting to see?" Elijah asked. "I have never known you to be the kind of man that gives up and surrenders. I have never known you to be the kind of man that backs down from a challenge. You are an overly loud, abrasive lummox of a man, but you fight until your last breath. This should be no different. In fact, you should be fighting harder than ever against these people. So I am going to ask you again, Purdue: What are we going to do about these so-called Visionaries?"

The hopelessness he had been feeling was dissipating, replaced by a newfound desire to stop those people from winning. The world really was at risk with those people around. No matter how they handled the threat, the Order of the Black Sun needed to band together. They might be the only ones that could keep the Visionaries from completely rewriting the past to forge the future that they controlled.

"We have to stop them."

"Yes, we do. But how?"

That was the question, and it was one that they needed to find the answer to.

∼

Purdue spent some time sitting in the vault room as the curator got back to work. He thought about how every single one of those artifacts had a story, not just from when it came from in history but also from how it was connected to the Order of the Black Sun. Every single item in that room had either been discovered or recovered by Purdue and his friends or another member of the Order of the Black Sun. All of their work and effort had yielded results. They had proof that their mission of protecting the past worked. Some people might complain about how they did it, but the fact of the matter was those relics were safer with them than they were with anyone else, especially considering what the Visionaries were up to.

People had come after those artifacts before, but usually it was to steal them or use the powers that some of those old items contained. He had never been up against an enemy that wanted nothing more than to see it all burn and would obviously do whatever they could to make sure that that happened. It was a whole different kind of fear. At least when his prizes had been taken before, there was a chance that he could get them back. With these people, the Visionaries, once those items were gone, then they were gone forever.

It was a threat unlike any that they had ever faced before and they were still only scratching the surface. They had come across a couple of the Visionaries themselves, but the rest were still out there, all still conspiring about how they were going to destroy history.

When Purdue started all of his expeditions around the globe, searching for treasure and adventure, it was all about seeking some thrills that he couldn't get anywhere else. It was a purely selfish thing, but now he realized that it wasn't about that anymore. He still got excited about those expeditions, but there was so much more on the line now than just his enjoyment. If they didn't stop the Visionaries, then so much of the world's history would be tarnished. It would be a catastrophe—and the Order of the Black Sun were the only ones that could stop it.

He hoped that he was ready for that, but the future was so uncertain.

EPILOGUE -

EPILOGUE
THE VISION IMPAIRED

Damon Meyer had never been angrier in his life. No one had ever dared to try to make a fool of him, let alone actually injure him. The Order of the Black Sun was becoming more and more of a problem, and despite his best efforts, the threat that they posed to the Visionaries persisted. He wanted them all dead and gone, along with all of their relics being scrubbed off the face of the earth. He wanted every trace of them wiped out and forgotten. There was no place for them in the future; he would be sure of that.

He stared at himself in the mirror and at the bandage that was wrapped around his skull, covering his left eye. The injury was still fresh, and according to some of the surgeons that he hired, the bullet had done a significant amount of damage to his eye, enough that he would never be able to see out of it again. That old breastplate had turned his own weapon against him and had maimed him for the rest of his life. It was disgusting, disgraceful, and he wished that the flames he had doused that armor with had actually worked. That would have saved his eyes.

When he initially came up with the plan to hurt the Order of the Black Sun, to bring them out with the new Third Triumvirate, he never expected that it would end the way that it had. He never thought that he could end up being hurt by them. Perhaps he had let his own hubris get the better of him.

As much as he hated to admit it, maybe David Purdue's threats toward the Visionaries should have been taken more seriously. The man had that trove of artifacts that he and his friends had collected, and if what the breastplate of Alexander did was any indication, then a lot of those pieces of trash might have actually had real power that could do some real harm. That piece of armor should have just been forgotten and lost forever; instead, it had taken his eye away.

"You don't look well, Damon." One of the Visionaries had seen fit to visit him in person, but he knew that she was just there to gloat and smirk at the sight of his injury. She found his humiliation to be amusing, obviously.

"I have certainly been better," Damon growled. He hated looking weak or vulnerable, so there was nothing worse than having one of his fellow Visionaries see his injury. They were looking down on him, pitying him, and he could not stand it. "But I will live. It is nothing that I can't handle."

"How did such a thing happen to you? How did you let them cut your eye out?"

"They didn't cut it out," Damon said. "The power of Alexander's armor turned my own bullet against me."

She laughed, and it was the most humiliating thing that Damon had ever heard. "Your own bullet? You shot yourself in the eye?"

"I told you...it was the power of the breastplate..."

"Or perhaps you are just a poor shot. I'm only teasing, Damon. You don't have to look so glum. I think it suits you. You always did have an asymmetrical face. Again, I'm just teasing."

Damon wanted to strangle her for the way she was speaking to him, but he had no grounds to actually put his hands on her. All that would do was get him excommunicated from the Visionaries. He had already suffered enough embarrassment. He didn't need to do anything that would bring about any more of it.

"We can't keep letting the Order of the Black Sun get in the way. If they do it enough, then some of our followers are going to lose faith. We can't have that. Their faith and their belief in our cause is the only way that we can move forward. We need the whole world to see the possibilities that we do."

"I know that," Damon said. Of course he did, and he was insulted that she felt like she had to remind him. "I would have put an end to it right there and then if not for that damned breastplate."

"That just sounds like an excuse."

"You can believe that if you want but considering that it took my eye from me...I think that it's more than that."

"The rest of the Visionaries had a meeting while you were out, losing your eye. We have come to the decision that we must put aside everything else that we are doing and focus solely on the destruction of the Order of the Black Sun. We cannot continue to try to move forward with our plans while they continue to sabotage all of our efforts. That will get us nowhere. This most recent debacle is proof of that."

"No."

"No? What do you mean *no*?"

"I mean that the rest of you should carry on as usual. There is no need to stall and delay, at least not on a wide scale. You all continue the work, and I will devote my time to making sure that they are no longer a problem."

"After what just happened—"

"This business with the Third Triumvirate and the breastplate of Alexander was nothing more than a miscalculation on my part, and a telling one at that. I will learn from it and not make the same mistakes. Besides, now I have more motivation than ever to make sure that they are all taken care of. After what they took from me, I want to take everything from them."

She seemed unsure at first, but he doubted that she or the other Visionaries would have a problem with his plan. They enjoyed being able to do as they wanted and having other people do things for them.

"Okay. You will have another chance before the rest of us step in."

"I appreciate it."

When she left, he looked into the mirror and started to pull off his bandages. He wanted to see it, how he looked after that bullet grazed his eye, after what they did to him with that old piece of armor. He pulled off the wrapping and stared at what was left of his left eye—a mangled, bloody eye socket and eyeball that was glazed over, with a gray iris that would never be able to see again.

Those people had nearly taken his vision away, but he still had one eye, more than enough to see the future that they were trying to make—a future where he would have vengeance on the ones that hurt him.

THE END

Made in the USA
Las Vegas, NV
26 November 2024